# Rainsong

*Stories*



PRATYAKSHA

*Translated from the Hindi by the author*

HARPER PERENNIAL

NEW YORK • LONDON • TORONTO • SYDNEY • NEW DELHI • AUCKLAND

HARPER PERENNIAL

First published in India in 2014 by Harper Perennial
An imprint of HarperCollins *Publishers*
HarperCollins *Publishers* India, Cyber City,
Building 10-A, Gurugram, Haryana-122002, India



The story 'Invisible Alley' translated by Reenu Talwar.

P-ISBN: 978-93-5029-761-2
E-ISBN: 978-93-5029-762-9

2 4 6 8 10 9 7 5 3



Typeset in 11/14 Minion Pro
by Jojy Philip, New Delhi 110 015

Printed and bound at
Replika Press Pvt. Ltd.

HarperCollins *Publishers*, Macken House, 39/40 Mayor Street Upper, Dublin 1, D01 C9W8, Ireland

# Contents

# Rainsong

Pratyaksha has published two collections of short stories in Hindi: *Jungle Ka Jadoo Til Til* (Bhartiya Jnanpith) and *Pahar Dopahar Thumri* (HarperCollins *Publishers* India). She received the Sonbhadra Katha Samman 2011 for the former. Her stories have been translated into many Indian languages, English and Norwegian. She won the Indo Norwegian Prize 'In Your Shoes' for her English story 'That I Be a Gannet' in 2012, which is being published in an anthology to be launched in Oslo this year. Her English poems have been published in *Pyrta* and *Everyday Poets*. They have also been longlisted for RLP award 2013 and published in their anthology *The Unsettled Winter*. She is currently working on a novel in English and on translation of international poets into Hindi. She was awarded the Krishna Baldev Vaid Fellowship for 2013. She lives in Gurgaon, India, and works full-time as chief manager finance with PowerGrid Corporation. She blogs at www.pratyaksha.blogspot.com.

# ONE

# *Friend*

A slow, whispering song, a bit of melody, floats by the lonely street, murmuring: 'Friend?'

Drunken, gyrating to a rhythm, a broken hiccup, a forgotten-forsaken tune born of the unison of breath, a fallen body, wet and hot, a caress in the dark, stealthily jumping in from the window, whispers: 'Have you seen the feet of air?' The trembling heat of the last particle on the fingertips, tipsy, and hiding and shrinking in a tizzy. Its stubborn innocence squeezes its eyes shut and mumbles: 'There's us, just us…' Like a warm kiss on the forehead, like the racing beat of a child's heart, sweet, so divinely sweet… God knows where it comes from, pulsing through the veins, invisible, nonexistent but still so real. Pulsing with the fragrance of a yellow champa flower in the dark of the night—friend?

# I Am Love

His voice came from far. Faintly, like the sound of pebbles falling into a deep well. After every word there was silence, like near a small pond where words echoed after long pauses. I was assailed by a sudden weary and painful yearning wrapped in a memory from childhood. Of a time spent by the pond in our backyard. We wore shirts and shorts, our knees were bruised from tumbling on the ground. We threw flat pebbles in the water and watched them skim its surface, bouncing. Often we would sit there until darkness fell.

His voice came to me straddling across all those years, across all the darkness in between, travelling through space and time and memory. Quiet and balanced, leisurely and thought out. Devoid of any panic or restlessness. As if those words and phrases were being formed in his mind for the very first time.

> *Listen carefully. Are you listening? When you are in love your goodness magnifies a thousand fold. If you are possessive, the possessiveness can reach that extreme state where you can kill someone for passion, or you can kill yourself. And if you are generous, no one can stop you from becoming a Sufi. And when you love as a Sufi, your beloved's good or bad, everything arouses only devotion in you. Your love expands to touch the horizon. There are no more boundaries.*

Har simt main dekhoon nazar aata hai ki tum ho
(*Whichever way I see, all I see is you.*)

He quoted Faraz, then said,

*I am planning to quit work in a few years. Do you remember that ancestral house of ours in that small town, where when you start walking on the courtyard, in order to go from its one end to the other, you walk almost a kilometre? You won't even begin to fathom when the courtyard of one house ends and that of another begins. The place is still the same. Just as there are no demarcations between courtyards, so there are no boundaries between peoples' homes; their lives merge into one another, and so everyone is an aunt, uncle granny, sister; it's all one big family. Everything is close by, even the cemetery. I want to spend the youth of my old age there. Maybe I can keep a few rabbits for pets. Some pigeons too. I might then begin to write as well. Not a love story, but the story of life. What do you say?*

*I will read Braudel and Stendhal. I will read life.*

His voice had travelled to some faraway land, but his words came loud and clear, their taste clean. It held an intense sort of yearning. It was forlorn, like a boy lost.

*Do you know I am in a sort of drunken stupor these days, intoxicated with myself? I have quit drinking. Do you remember those days when we would drink every evening? What days they were. Now I keep drinking myself; I remain immersed in myself. Late in the night, I walk the streets. In the dim, twinkling lights of the rain-drenched streets, I watch the city rush by. I watch the blurred, anxious faces of people. I watch the lost, barren faces of women wearily returning home, and I watch the cheap call girls standing under lampposts round street corners, waiting for customers, with their garishly made, vacant faces and vulgar clothes, and obscenely shaking their bums and making sluttish gestures. I watch a slice of life from outside the windows; the depressing interiors swathed in dim, yellow light, and think why life is the way it is. Why? Why is life such a caricature all the time? What do you say?*

Then, without waiting to hear what I had to say, he began to laugh. His laughter was that of a child who had aged prematurely. Then just as suddenly, he started hiccupping. I panicked. Listen, drink some water. Count seven swallows. He replied, 'Why don't I drink seven swallows of myself. What do you say?' I realized this habit of his still remains. Of getting an endorsement for every sentence he says.

We were speaking after four years. In these four years, we had not existed for each other. Then suddenly, while rummaging through an old diary, I had stumbled upon a yellow note pressed between the pages that had his name written three times and a different number against each. I had dialled the first number. A woman had picked up and informed me in a cold voice that he no longer lived there. At the second number, he had picked up, and without getting surprised or without complaining or even asking for or giving an explanation for the years of silence, he had begun talking, as if we had left our conversation midway only yesterday.

*You know my life is like some costly wine or an expensive cigarette. Every swig or puff …*

Then he took a pause. A pause so long that I feared the phone had got disconnected.

*Forget it. Listen, the last time I went to my village and stayed there for a fortnight, there was no electricity. I would sit in the night by the light of a kerosene lamp, holding some book in my hand and thinking of distant places I have never been to.*

*To be able to live in an apple orchard, to pick fruits all day long, eat some bread in the night and fall off to sleep, pleasantly tired... If life became so simple, do you think the mind would still be so restless? Where does mind get its resources? From whom? From what? Will my mind, my heart and my intellect remain forever hungry? Will I always remain poor—starved, parched and naked?*

*I would go to the fields in the day, sit under the shade of some old tree and look at the freshly ploughed land, talk to the simple farmers, put my feet in the wet, warm soil and feel the goodness of it seeping through my soles, fill my lung with the cleanest air that God could provide. You know to breathe like that, full and deep, is also a kind of sensual pleasure.*

*But the village folks would look at me sceptically as if I was high on some dope. Maybe they even laughed at me behind my back with disdain. Okay, tell me, where would I find a life that was simple materially, mentally and emotionally as well?*

Then his voice tapered off to a whisper, as if he were explaining things to himself.

*Listen, in the night someone should be close by, the warmth of a human body, even if you don't touch it. But having the assurance that if you desired the touch, you had around someone who could be touched with love, affection and calmness, who would confirm your sensations of being alive...*

He fell silent. I too remained quiet, holding my breath.

*In the long, lonely hours of the night, I touch myself, caressing my body, seeking the warmth of life. It is like lying in the coffin, alone. Cold and lifeless. Sometimes I want to buy a woman, just to be able to lie next to her. Maybe that will make me go to sleep. Then, as if erasing all that he had said, he laughed emptily and said, See, what nonsensical things I have been talking about.*

He had then disconnected the phone abruptly. This was all we spoke about that day. Somebody told me later on that his wife had left him, and that he fibs shamelessly and drinks like a fish. He has become a poster for some worthless piece of trash. If anyone needs to see how a guy can stoop inconceivably low, all he needs to do is to see him. The person who told me all this had grimaced with distaste.

I had not saved his number from that crumpled yellow note. Maybe I loved him too much, regardless of his strengths and flaws. But I was not a Sufi. Maybe I was not even a human being like him.

Whenever these days I take a puff or have a drink, I don't know why, but his memory unwittingly creeps in. In place of that yellow note, I have kept, very carefully, the obituary cutting. Sometimes when I am drunk enough, I take it out and look at it. His face is grainy, but if you look closely, you can see the eyes, bright and questioning, asking: 'Why is life a fucking caricature all the time?

## *Lonely in the Dark*

There was a garden, filled with sun. There was a room too, with no walls. The garden had a blue roof. There was greenery in the room. The woman thought it was heaven, inside and outside. Thinking thus made her intensely happy. And as she said this, a lonely bird took a sharp flight into the blue sky.

As the train rushed past, her body leaning towards the window swayed in a rhythm: have to go far away, sweetheart, a faraway land. Squatting along the open door, a basket at her feet, the village woman's face is like that of an Egyptian queen's—the same hauteur. So out of place here. She lights up a beedi and looks with a calm gaze at me. As our eyes meet, she smiles. But does she really smile? By the time one is able to catch the end of the rope, to understand the smile, the train vanishes. The sharp, fast wind brings a tear to my eyes. To sit without a roof overhead, to sit without leaning against a wall makes one feel so orphaned. So lonely in the dark, so, so lonely…

The world is so wrong.

Or maybe it's you who's wrong? His voice is laced with the happiness of laughter. He looks askance, then stretches his hands.

Shall I touch you? Hold you?
What? It is the same happiness as that of your laughter.
You are a little bit crazy.
I am a little bit sane.
She closes her eyes, thinks of something, then proffers her face,
Here.

The man becomes sad, very sad. As if darkness has fallen everywhere. But he kisses the woman with a strange sort of courage, first her forehead, then her lips. Then, in an anxious sort of panic, he kisses her on her lips again and again. He can't trace the happiness of that laughter any more. A sort of deep, dense sorrow floods him. He whispers slowly, Oh, so much sadness.

The woman says, It is so dark and you tend to think such strange thoughts. Then she says, My fellow traveller.

The bird returns from its sortie and asks, So is this the world? Only so much. You had trapped me in such an illusion until now. Which garden, what room? Which train, where does it go?

# *Take Care of Me*

The day passes, a shadow quivering, shrinking on the wall. The shadow treads nearby, the night remains, the dream in the eyes passes by. Flowers of fire bloom in the desert. The souls of the feet are cracked, the journey never ends. The day passes by, so does the breath, and gathers on the chest. Then darkness melts in the night, just like that, for no reason at all.

In the dark of the night, a circle of light flowers slowly. An inkpot, a fountain pen and copy and a postcard in between books with well-formed, beautiful letters. A trace of turmeric on the chipped teacup, a comb, wooden, bought the last time for two hundred rupees from the handicraft market where I had seen such knick-knacks like cloth birds, ribbons and tattoos. A voice sang from behind…

> *o laal meri pat rakhiyo bala jhoole laalan, sindari da sevan da sakhi shabaz kalandar…*

His voice was melted honey. And his eyes were viscous and intoxicating. The voice soared with such a lilt that it felt it would take one's heart along. It rose in delicate, layered tones, like flavoured fragrant nut shavings on an aromatic betel leaf. Listening to it was like losing one's senses, one's heart.

The band of gypsies left in the middle of the night. A peep from the window shows a ghostly ragtag group disappearing beneath the moonshine with all baggage on a ramshackle cart. Maybe all this is a figment of imagination, a page out of a forgotten book read long ago. One returns again and again, touches the pages of the book, and smells the day. The heart cries in a stupor and thinks or sees God knows what from those eyes.

# TWO

## *One Afternoon, You Won't Believe*

When we talk, the air between us flows like water. You won't believe this, but many times I have seen tiny fish, bright orange ones, swimming across sentences, diving and soaring, flashing left then right with such speed, like lightning. You complain:

'You are not listening to me.'

I smile, not at what you are saying, but because a naughty fish has just swum past, nibbling at my ears. Butterflies too fly at times in the air between us, and sometimes the curtains across the windows whisper. So many of our conversations hang like tiny bells from their hem. On the table in the saucers and plates, along with the leftover rice and dal, the taste of our fingers too lingers.

You won't believe. The shadow that falls on the wall when sunlight streams in, its fragrance is also one with the atmosphere. The cigarette smoke that wafts up from your fingers up to my face pauses near the curtains. I am hardly a passive smoker. I do not nag you to quit smoking; I like the smell of cigarette smoke. I smile and you say: 'You are not listening to me.'

I am really not listening to you. I am bursting with happiness. I am talking to myself. The light behind the curtain peeps and withdraws. In this game, the room assumes a new shape, and the things in it acquire a new meaning, as if they now belong to a different plane.

But sometimes something heavy straddles my chest, which makes me as light as a cotton flower. Then small sufferings cower away in the dark. My mind soars in the universe, as if I could unravel all the mysteries of the world—underwater, in the desolate expanse of a desert, over the barren, rocky mountains, in godforsaken places—and in a primitive ritual, turn my face towards the sun in devotion.

The curtain sways, the light laughs, the darkness smiles. You say:

'You are not listening to me.'

You won't believe it, but this time I am really listening to you.

# Five Tales

## *One: Lighthouse*

Why are your lips so sour? the man asks cruelly.

And your heart? The woman's face is hard. She must have been beautiful when she was young, a bit like Leela Naidu, high forehead and a bit of a widow's peak.

The man is drunk on some cheap alcohol and the acerbic intoxication makes everything appear to him harsh and acidic. Bloody hell dope, he murmurs while biting on a piece of dried fish. On the wall in front is a black and white picture of Alicia Markova; the play of light and shadow lights up her face and sets it aglow. and The colours dilute the stark distinctions of the image. The woman no longer likes to dangle midway. There are no games any more.

She puts her feet up and curls up in the easy chair, looking out of the window, savouring the dark. There is nothing outside, not a soul. Only dense, ink-blue darkness. The woman keeps watching the dark emptiness, the absence of light. She listens, as if hypnotized, to the distant rumble of waves. When she was young she had read the story of a girl, in *Look Alive*, who lived in a lighthouse. On a stormy night, alone and terrified, she had mustered up the courage to face the lashing of sea water to climb up the ladder to light the lamp inside it. The woman thinks: how far is the mainland, how terrifying the storm; and trapped in the lighthouse, she is yet to light the lamp.

The man has rolled down on the rug in a drunken stupor. The bottle is empty. The fishbones make an abstract design on the white bone-china plate, singing the death song of plump saltwater fish. The man snores and trembles in an inebriated sleep, turning on his side and falling into oblivion once again. The woman rests her face on her arms and remembers a long-forgotten song left on the lonely beach of a bygone time—a tune that belonged to a wandering gypsy, an uncertain yearning, a quest which even she can't put a finger on. A blunt hurt rises and sinks in her heart, a wail catches in her throat, a breath pauses in her chest. The lighthouse lies inert in the dark.

Not the lighthouse, but the search for a Chinese house; a search, which always remains unfulfilled, rings out in the song. Paulo Conte sings in his rough, many-timbred gravel and silk voice—*La Casa Cinese.*

## *Two: Fish and Happiness*

Have you ever seen a hook entangled in a fish's lung? The more the fish sinks in water to get rid of the hook, the deeper the hook gets embedded in its body. Just like the fish hook, a nail has sunk deep into my heart, and with every breath, it twinges. How can one go on with the daily chore of living with such heaviness. It is as if my heart has been shred into pieces. The woman keeps saying these things to herself all the time. Sometimes, she talks to the shadow that flits from the wall to the roof and from the roof to the skylight and then to the window. Sometimes, placing her palms on her chest and listening to its beat, she engages herself in intimate conversations.

The woman is simple. She views everything around her with a simple gaze. Even if something complex or twisted comes along, she immediately smoothes and straightens it out as far as possible.

The man is not simple. He is twisted, like a jalebi. And when he is not twisted, he is simple, because it serves his purpose to be so. And the woman, however straightforward and uncomplicated she may be, she intuitively understands this trait of the man, in the manner in which a woman has hunches about things they don't really grasp properly. Despite all this, their life moves on as if in an interplay of the simple and the dense, of his happiness and her sorrow. Even at the peak of happiness, a river of sadness sweeps the woman away. Then everything, this shanty, these trees, the livestock, the pet cat, the shed, everything floats on the water. The dream and togetherness, the whole fabric of being floats like a tiny twig in the turbulent waters. The man watches, detached. The woman thinks: is he with me? When he looks at me, can he see my sorrow? What does he see in me? Does he see anything at all? Does he see my suffering?

The man gobbles up the lunch ravenously and thinks: a beedi after my meal. Then, under the open blue sky, he lies down on the cot, cradling his head on his arms, and draws in a breath of contentment and pleasure. The woman potters inside the shanty, scrapes out the leftovers from the utensils, a handful of boiled rice. Eating it with onion and red chilli, she sadly ponders. Carrying a heavy weight on her chest, she moves about the tiny space, her feet heavy and clumsy. She pauses for a second, exhales then inhales, sighs and looks around at the four walls. Everything is cold and numb.

She wishes that her heart too would be simple, that she were not so sensitive, that she wouldn't think too much, that she wouldn't constantly be plagued by the question of existence, the meaning of life. That she would not take to heart this situation of to be or not to be. That she would be happy just eating rice and curry, and stay content in the company of this insensitive man. That her mind would be like the fleeting, flying sparrow that would be happy pecking at seeds. What would the sparrow be thinking? Not burdened by memory nor anxious about the future, and neither worrying about the present going waste, nor of being hurt over an existence slowly seeping out.

The woman thinks for a second, then pushes the red glass bangles up her thin, dry wrists and takes out the vegetable cutter. She cleans the fish and grinds a mustard paste on the stone grinder, flavouring the spice with a few drops of tears. In the night, the man eats rice with fish curry and belches with satisfaction. Today the fish was cooked to perfection.

## *Three: Life Is So beautiful*

When she had bumped into me the first time, I had felt pissed off. She should look where she is going. Without paying any attention to me, she had picked up the envelopes and hurried away. Then I found her just ahead of me at Spencer's. The same steel grey hair. Today they hung around her shoulders. She took a lot of time to take money out of her wallet and do the calculation. I was hopping on one foot to the other impatiently. Thanks to her, a full five minutes had been wasted.

After a week, we met in a lingerie shop. Sweeping away all the lacy bright lingerie, she picked up a sports bra. Before Manipur's Carmen emptied the whole carton on the counter, she picked up a white speedo with a practised hand and marched towards the payment counter. I loafed around for some time with Carmen, flirted with her, complimenting her on her straight, brown hair contrasting with her smooth, pale cheeks and her mascaraed lashes. Carmen kept blushing, although it was our old routine.

'Shall I take out the sexy black for madam?' she teased flirtatiously. Carmen knew that madam never wore black. In the beginning, madam came alone to this shop, then I began to accompany her. I would wonder sometimes what would happen if I landed up alone here. Would these girls throw me out of the premises? Or would the six-foot tall, slender, willow-like owner of the shop breeze in from her plush room with a, 'Hello, I am Niharika, can I be of any assistance?'

Lately, I had hit upon the novel idea of giving myself birthday gifts. I had bought dozens of night dresses, accessories and knick-knacks for K. After that initial bravado, I had begun to enjoy shopping for her.

Having made the payment, I sauntered into Sub Zero, and once again she was standing across. Holding a three-scoop cone, she was eating like a child, eating less and spilling more. The minute her eyes met with mine, she blushed with embarrassment. Then the other day, I sprained my ankle in the jogger's park and fell in a heap. In the foggy twilight of early morning, she was one of the two people who came running. I had pulled a tendon and was advised crepe bandage and fifteen days' bedrest.

On the fourth day, K went to office. My day went horribly. On the fifth day, *she* arrived. Straight grey blunt hair, an oversize steel grey pullover hanging down to her knees, blue slacks and a maroon muffler around her shoulders. All right, so this was K's promised surprise. She had come with two sunflowers.

Shall I read you something? She held up a slender volume of Seamus Heany's poetry.

*There are the mud-flowers of dialect/And the immortelles of perfect pitch/ And that moment when the bird sings very close/ To the music of what happens.*

Then,

*As a child, they could not keep me from wells/And old pumps with buckets and windlasses./I loved the dark drop,/the trapped sky, the smells of waterweed, fungus and dank moss.*

and

*And here is love/Like a tinsmith's scoop/Sunk past its gleam/ In the meal bin*

Her voice was lyrical, a little layered—husky as if from long years of smoking. She left as suddenly, without a word about future visits. The sixth day went by, then seventh. On the eighth day, as I was about to pour some hot broth from the thermos to eat, the bell rang. She entered along with the cold breeze. Her face was flushed with the chill from outside. Without any greeting, she pulled a chair, pulled out a book from her bag. No poems today, she said. 'Do you keep any music? I gestured towards the stereo deck.' She got up silently, played Schubert's '*Ave Maria*', returned to the chair and immersed herself in her book.

I seethed with indignation: what sort of a woman is she? I tried to be gracious and asked: 'Would you like something?'

'No, no, it is all right.'

She looked up, then went back to her book. I tried to peep in and see what she was reading, then became restless and vacant, then a bit annoyed. So she helped me that day, but that does not give her any right to come here like this. I don't need anyone. We listened to Schubert then Haydon, silently, without exchanging a word. Then, as breezily as she had come, she departed.

At night, I complained like a child to K. 'She is some eccentric, crazy woman. Why does she come?' I blabbered and K kept smiling in response. My ankle healed, but a stubborn pain persisted. Despite that, my next few weeks were hectic. I went on a tour for ten days. When I returned, K left for a week. I lounged alone in the house, half-hearted and dispirited. I spent the Saturday varnishing the cane swing. On Sunday, I went unannounced, with a bottle of Red Zinfandel and a spray of blue orchids. She was ill at ease for a moment, then she gestured at the cushions lying scattered on the orange rug.

She brought two wine glasses. 'This year I will complete sixty-seven,' she said, handing me a glass. 'When will you start jogging?' she asked randomly. We talked for two hours, without touching upon Schubert or Heaney. This time we talked cinema and laughed a lot. Maybe it was the wine.

Life is so beautiful, isn't it? Her face, lined and wrinkled, was flushed with a beauty. Truly.

*K had told me some days ago that she lived alone. Her husband was no more. She had gone to the US to visit her son, and as soon they arrived there, he had met with an accident, one of those highway tragedies. There were friends, but it was a strange, unknown city, and above all, her pain and suffering knew no boundaries. It swept across her emotional emptiness. She returned. Since then she has lived alone. So brave. Such is life, bloody unjust but beautiful.*

## *Four: Bathtub, Man and the Caterpillar*

Oh what a thankless, hopeless life this is. The man bites on dust from the dilapidated road as he ponders. There is a row of one-storey shops: Ma Ambe Tent House, Snow-White laundry, pure vegetarian meal at Mahaveer Restaurant, Sai Photocopier, Mittal Chemicals and Guddu Pappi Dee Gaddi, and to ward of evil eye a bunch of green chilies strung atop a lemon. The life amidst such exteriors is so predictable. Everyone is carrying the burden of living like a yoked bull.

The woman, however, thinks of colours. Morning, noon, night. All day long. While waking up and drifting into sleep. So much so that her eyes get tired and red-rimmed, and then she can only see in black and white. But will thinking so much change everything? Has it ever happened? So what if she thinks with a devil-may-care attitude. The woman's heart beats a tattoo, an echo sounds within, in all its glory.

The rag-seller has a pile of trash in his shop, broken stuff, old and ramshackle, the paint peeling off them. And amidst all the junk prettily sits an old enamel bathtub that Josan had brought for his beloved Matilda in 1923. Blue-eyed Josan and green-eyed Matty. And when she played on the piano, *'I won't say I will but I won't say I won't'*, how Josan looked at her, completely enamoured. But what does the man care about Josan. In this small backwater town, the Christian cemetery is now obscured with tall elephant grass. A flock of lamb and sheep strays into it sometimes through a hole in the wall. Then the tiny bells tied around their necks tinkle a sweet melody, somewhat like the sound of the piano. The shepherd rests on the cemetery's broken boundary wall, gazing at the clouds in the blue sky.

In the big courtyard of that small house, the bathtub is

installed in one corner with great ceremony. The woman giggles uncontrollably. 'Oh gosh! Who is supposed to take bath in this? Me, you or our brood of chicken.' She doubles up with mirth. She laughs so much that tears sparkle in her eyes. And in the tears, her rainbow dreams reflect iridescently. The man smiles bashfully. Scratching his ears, he lowers his head, then laughs. Sitting on the edge of the bathtub, he laughs. 'Got this for you, who else,' he adds defiantly, still smiling. The man's heart fills up with the inexplicable emotion brought on by doing something unpredictable in an extremely predictable world. His heart swells with exuberance. The woman's laughter brims with sweetness and joy. The small corner of the courtyard is dappled with sun and happiness. The caterpillar at the bottom of the bathtub crawls a little further towards the shaded coolness of its base.

## *Five: Myopic love*

The side frame of the glasses were thick tortoise shell. The lenses were also thick. They were sturdy, but had one great deficiency. They made Munni's eyes, behind them, look like an owl's, thick, bulging and wide, protruding from their sockets. However much she practised looking at herself in the mirror or squinting to make them look narrow, it slipped her mind at the right moment to narrow them. When she would remember, the moment would have passed. Munni loved sexy, narrow, slit eyes. But what she wanted was another story. Preferences and wants are one thing and reality, another. They give each other a wide berth. Munni knew all this. But this knowledge didn't help. The idea of narrow, upturned eyes remained secure in her dreams while the thick tortoise-shell glasses remained firmly in their place.

It was not that Munni wanted only one thing. She had a list of other ambitions too. For example, she wanted a fair complexion, a sharp nose and one tiny black mole anywhere on her face. In reality, Munni wore a wheatish complexion, her nose swept across her face, and she did have a tiny black mole, but it struggled for attention along the hairline on her temporal lobe.

So while her wish list remained as it is, Munni grew up in years. Her glasses became thicker. To be fair though, her complexion trotted towards fairness, thanks to all the *multani mitti*, cream and turmeric face masks she applied. And so far as the mole was concerned, her yearning for it was cruelly discarded, like a stupid childhood game.

And so far as the nose was concerned, its sweep across the face developed a strangely sensuous spread, so deadly that all the eligible boys of the neighbourhood felt their hearts slipping on it more than once. But every time the thick glasses held their hearts at bay. Munni grew up waiting for a knight in shining armour to discover her. But slowly and steadily, as the barren years passed her by, she became convinced of the age-old notion that men don't make passes at a woman with glasses. So be it.

But who has ever been able to block the way of destiny, coincidence, or even strange occurrences. Making a mockery of the dreadfully high myopic power of twelve, an eligible suitor not only appeared on the horizon but is believed to have had a head-on collision with Munni in which her tortoise-shell glasses were smashed to smithereens. Munni is said to have smiled across her myopic fog, and an arrow pierced the suitor's heart through a fine hole. Love is nothing but a game of hormones and pheromones. So the game began like a grand upheaval.

The couple that you see across the window, gazing into each other's eyes without the barrier of spectacles are Munni and her spouse. I had told you earlier that the hubby's power is much higher than Munni's. Both of them delicately take off their glasses, blow into the glasses a warm breath, wipe them with yellow flannel and then keep them aside. If one has to look into the eyes of one's beloved, why should the glasses come in between? He is not able to see Munni's bulging eyes and Munni can't see his hooked nose. A river of sweet love begins to flow between them. In its spray of myriad colours and in the haziness of their myopic gaze, their faces blur and soften. Pheromones and myopia trot a merry three-legged race.

# *After the Night*

Nirmal rests her head on her elbow and looks at a corner of the wall. It is hot and humid and dark. The palla of her sari is spread out on the floor like a blue river in the dark night. Her body and mind melt. The heat prickles her waist. Still her heart brims over: To lie this way, to feel the roughness of someone's toe nails on the soles. To feel without touching…

In the dark, her eyes laugh and, from their corners, light rains down as if flashing a firefly's laughter. Amiya lies flat on his back, his head on his arms. He hums slowly and knows without seeing that she laughs.

Nirmal says, 'And then?'

Amiya looks at the ceiling and sighs, 'What then? Nothing really.'

The room is suddenly filled with his voice, as if it was never empty. Riding on his voice, contentment has spread like wind and moonlight in the room. That bookshelf, this table, that one lonely plant. The room is no more the room it used to be. Amiya stretches his hands and touches Nirmal's arms once. In the middle of the night, the man who lies thus is hardly like Amiya. When did Amiya ever have this deep collected sense of contentment. This is some other time within this time, some other room within this room. Isn't it so?

Nirmal says haltingly, 'Do you know when I was learning music, I felt like a bird riding on the waves of my voice, as if my soul had sprouted wings. Now I feel if I sqeeze my soul and spread it out to dry, my voice will fall down like autumn leaves. And I here, in this room, with you, without any sound and without my soul, just like this, silent, soundless and soulless, will be buried.

In the midst of this, Amiya gets up, sips a mouthful of water, then comes back and sits besides her, saying slowly, 'Morning is still hours away.' In his voice, still lies the whole night unspent.

'Nirmal.'

Somebody calls from far. The beckoning is like a thin wire stretched as if the body is separated from the voice. In that voice, there is smoke and suffering. Somebody seeks me in pain. She awakens dizzily to find the sari wrapped around her throat. She gets up embarrassed. The books sitting on the shelf look at her solemnly. Loneliness reverberates in the room. The sound of her breath pulses. The string of the tanpura is broken, the drummer has run away and the intimate tale has been converted into a public story.

She puts a fallen eyelash on the mount of her palm and blows at it, eyes closed, and all the words between them are blown away to smithereens.

Amiya asks, 'Why do you become so sad often?'

Nirmal sits on her haunches, her arms around her knees. Her body sways slowly, like a young girl who is learning the tables. Her happiness overwhelms her and she asks, 'Do you know…?' Amiya's face is calm as if a light has been lit up inside it suddenly. His voice has so much love. 'Yes, tell me all.'

'The child inside you, I can forgive it a million crimes...'

'And the adult inside me? What about him?'

'I hate him intensely,' Nirmal's voice flattens when saying this.

Amiya hums unaware, '*Tum jo mil gaye ho toh aisa lagta hai ke jahaan mil gaya...*'

Then he turns smilingly at her. 'The night is still...'

Nirmal adds softly, 'Still not over...'

In the dark dense night, their laughters dance in unison.

## *The Eye of the Tiger*

The eye of the tiger turns inside once.
You are not allowed to laugh, her voice is serious.
But I can't help laughing.
Then I am sorry.

Somebody bombards you with snow the moment you enter a hot water spring. Far away, a column of mules, staggering with load, walk in a file in the shadows of the mountains, without green grass, without any probability of it or even the expectation.

'Why do you want to change me?'

Today I have worn a colourful floral sari, with so many flowers that everyone comes to say, 'Today there is so much of sunshine, it feels like it's the season for butterflies.'

It is foggy outside though, and I don't want to say anything to you. As if the period of hibernation has begun. Although I have always felt good in winters. In winters, life seems like it's just commenced, there are so many miracles and wonders to be anticipated yet.

While driving through dense fog in the night, the fog light bounces back to the windscreen and shatters into a million little pieces. I stop the car by the roadside and wipe the windscreen, and in a minute of play, make a face. In the uplifted brow of the face that looks back at me from the rear-view mirror, there is a sense of wonderment. Water and vapour together blur the image even before it is properly formed.

Two persons, sitting covered in coarse blankets by the roadside, warm their hands on the fire lit by burning trash. They turn to look at me. The work on the Metro rail is stalled. Once the fog lifts, the work will resume; sparks from the welding will fall on to the dust, a blue warmth frozen for a moment.

But the winter does not like those people, just as they do not like it. Warm clothes and complete houses can shield them from the spear of cold winds which makes their bones freeze and makes their children's noses run and fingers go numb. The necessities which are so elementary, where do they disappear and why? You won't understand anything. You will just say, 'You're not permitted to laugh,' and I will say,

'Listen, can you see the eye of the tiger? I can see it, but why do I see it?'

# THREE

## The Invisible Alley

A sudden gust of wind and russet leaves slowly float down from the tree, one by one. Those standing under it—Farrukhzad, Nusra Bi, Hamdu, Kubra, Humra, Afsaan, Rasool Badruddin, all the children, wizened old men and women—have composed their faces, for the photograph, into a ceremonial seriousness. The suddenness with which the leaves fall on hair, caps and scarves and their touch makes everyone smile. A few of them look up in surprise, and after a moment of laughter, collect themselves again, stare into the camera with resoluteness, and with curiosity, their eyes mirroring the brilliant morning sunshine.

Nazim clicks two photographs. One, with laughing faces looking up at the sudden shower of russet leaves and lit up with mirth, and the other, a serious, slightly sad picture with faces that have borne the brunt of life.

Right at the moment when Nazim was clicking the luminous photograph with the russet leaves, another photograph was being clicked, from behind, from behind where the people stood. This photograph shows everyone's backs; only Nazim can be seen from the front, working his camera.

The stranger does not know that behind the crowd of people in the photograph Nazim took is the hazy form of a person who is standing a little apart, who has his eye to the camera and is clicking a photograph of the photograph being clicked.

Her beautiful face blooming on a hunchbacked body disturbs people. At once so beautiful and so ugly…? Such beauty is also such a curse! The simultaneous comprehension of both the facts arouses an alarming disbelief in people. They turn back and look again and again, then shiver with revulsion and turn away.

She says, 'The river that flows in the city…'

A harried Hamdu says, 'Which river? We only have a lake here.'

On Kubra's pretty face, carrying the weight of tons of unhappiness, a mysterious smile begins to play. Slowly she turns, and with her back towards Hamdu, she says, 'There is a river…there for the one who wants to see it…'

After that, when Kubra would suddenly turn towards Hamdu, her palms would splay, as if water were flowing through her fingers. As if tears were uncontrollably flowing from her eyes, and had been flowing all through her life. For years she was a whore in a whorehouse, but never managed to get even one client. She spent her day making rotis in the kitchen. Kubra has been smouldering since then. Slowly. For so many years.

Eyes closed, Kubra soaks in the scent of cinnamon mixed with Hamdu's sweat. Hamdu hugs Kubra's hunched back to his chest. Kubra thinks, it's true, really true, that someone has such a warm body. Like what she had seen in the forest, rising and falling in slow rhythm, falling from leaves. A sight so beautiful that Kubra could have died seeing it. She saw, yet quickly she had moved away. That is how the body, becoming water, flows like a river. Her palms move from her breasts to her belly, wave upon wave.

It continues to snow outside, from between the gaps in the wooden slats, through the oil cloth, the mad, cold wind wanders in. The flames of the hearth keep blackening the wooden beams of the roof. God knows how many years of soot is accumulated there. This is Kubra's first winter inside the scratchy warmth of a blanket.

'Oh God,' her breath whispers slowly.

The foolish girl begins to cry again over the memory of some old hurt.

Nazim watches silently. A fly hovers over the wooden bench. There is a nip in the air. After many days, the sun has uncovered its face today and, although weak, sunshine spreads everywhere. There are dirty heaps of snow on the sides of the street. Workmen have cleared it this morning with spades. There is only this one street in town, Shahraah; the rest are lanes. This portion of the street is the most populated one. Right opposite is the kehwa ghar, from where a concoction of voices rises and escapes in a chatter through the windows together with the fragrance of kehwa and kebabs, and lingers awhile in the air. Right next to the kehwa ghar is the kitchen where one can get the most amazing shorba, korma, kebabs and pulav. On good days, Nazim has often brought maleeda and khajur in a paper bag for Farrukhzad.

On one side of the kehwa ghar is the Aj Zehra bank, and on the other side the library. The library is a domed building near the lake that also has a lavishly equipped reading room for those fond of reading. The books are from all over, the story of Gilgamesh, tales of Assurbanipal, Ibn al-Nadeem's

*Al-fihrist*, Abu-al Hasan's *Madin al Zawahiri* or *Maruz adh dhahab*, Sulaym Ibn Qais's *Kitaab*, the Quran and the Hadees. There are also old documents and calligraphy, silver and bronze coins, old disintegrating tomes, maps, and God alone knows what else.

Nazim's world is different from that world. However, the kehwa ghar beckons to him now and then. Especially today, when the wind is cold and piercing, and the warmth inside the kehwa ghar appears to be like the warmth of a cosy dream. If only some money were to come his way, a crisp nankhatai and steaming hot kehwa...

On the wooden box is an ancient pinhole camera. Right in front of that is a wooden chair. Next to it is a wooden bench with the paper and tray of chemicals lying on it—an instant dark room. There is also a faded square box made of vinyl, once upon a time red, now of some nondescript colour. It has an aluminum strip on it and a bolt, also a tiny lock.

Hands thrust deep into his brown overcoat, Nazim gazes at the street. It runs straight for about half-a-kilometre, then veers to the left behind a hillock and then suddenly disappears. Behind the hillock, the town ends. Nazim's beard flutters in the wind. The tip of his nose is slowly turning red in the cold. There is a dead fish-like sadness in his brown, red-rimmed eyes. Until a few years ago, he used to earn well. He was able to take Farrukhzad out, buy her dried fruit and ear hoops. In those days, many people would come to get their photograph taken. Old men wearing their karakuls, children with red cheeks bruised from the cold, old women in their hijabs, and sometimes, very rarely, a shy nervous young girl.

In this small town, for the longest time, Nazim was the only photographer. He had himself made his camera from an old wooden box. It had taken many days of hard work and strategizing to get the distance between the pinhole and the film at the back of the box right. Then the cardboard lever and the cover, he had made made from Ammi's old black burqa.

Nazim had a good eye. He was able to see things which did not show on the surface. He could discern the worlds hidden behind people's faces. From the pupils of their eyes and between the lines on their faces, he could read their inner secrets. And whenever he took a photograph, he clicked all those hidden worlds along with the visages that held them. Many a time, people would be amazed how Nazim had managed to capture a moment of happiness, when they themselves scarcely know or understood it. They would be filled with a strange sense of unease, as if something had been nailed inside them, as if something they had been hiding from their own selves had become apparent in Nazim's work.

The photographs would so appear on the rough paper that their fringes would be rubbed off. The sharp edges of features would soften in such a way that it would seem as if someone had wiped away the furrows with a light hand. The gaze would seem to go as far inside as it went outside. When someone asked Nazim how he managed to click such pictures, he would pretend that he hadn't understood what was being talked about.

The lake close to the library reflects pines, conifers, a blue sky and also the blue dome of the library. On its other shore, a flock of ducks and water-fowl descends. On the side that faces the street, wrought-iron benches are laid out in a neat row. When it is sunny, old women carrying paperbags full of walnuts and pine-nuts sit there with their children. Wrapped in woollens, the children play at the edge of the lake, exhaling vapour from their mouth. Their cheeks and lips have been so badly bruised by the sharp cold wind that they may even begin to bleed. Very often one of the grandmothers brings her darling grandchild to Nazim to get a photograph clicked.

Nazim sits on his wooden bench on the other side of the street and keeps an eye on the goings-on across it. Something snaps deep inside him. He feels there is a stranger living inside him, whom he has never met, and whom he may not even have the desire to meet. A heaviness settles on his chest. Something rises from the waters of the lake and enters deep inside him. Is that fear or something else? He does not know.

Nazim feels as if something stale is rotting inside him, like the smell of clothes left soaking in water for too long. A pair of scared, wet, drowning eyes begin to burn again into his back. He feels as if Dilyaar's corpse is always weighing down his shoulders. Only that one moment. Washed in hopelessness from head to foot, Nazim desperately wants to return to the time before that moment and begin his life once again. A pure and clean life.

Sometimes he wishes to run away into those fir and pine forests on the other shore of the lake. Sometimes he wants to take pictures, irrational pictures of the books in the library and the life-sized almirahs, pictures of the old woman, the wrinkles on whose face are so innumerable that her eyes shine though them like sparks from a fire. He wishes, for once, to walk out into the street, go beyond the hillock, just keep walking, and in case he returns, to be able to walk into the kehwa ghar as if he were a stranger in town. He wishes to say to Nusra bi, who owns the kehwa ghar, 'Come on, phoophi.

Get me the best of whatever you have in those jars and galli pots.' And then to jingle the coins in his pouch, look at the other patrons with intimacy and say, 'Gentlemen, please eat and drink whatever you like, it is on me.' He wishes to look at Kubra's pretty face and laugh without any reason, to let the shine on Farrukhzad's face light up his heart. He wishes there were no dark shadow looming over his heart, there were no moonless nights.

Nazim's shoulders droop. He wishes to burrow into the wet earth and hide, all alone.

Nibbling a piece of goat cheese, Nazim runs his fingers over the vinyl box. On the tree behind the wooden bench hang all the photographs that people got clicked but, due to some strange reason, have forgotten to take with them. All those photographs, dangling on a rope tied between two branches, flutter like flags in the wind. Nazim does not throw them away. They stay with him, the people in the photographs, fluttering in the wind: old men with hennaed hair; that very young boy whose moustache had hardly sprouted yet and in whose throat it seemed as if a bird hopped time and again; that blue-eyed man whose face had the purity of an angel, and the one with the enormous, dacoit-like moustaches who had shaken his finger at Nazim and warned him that the mole on his nose must not show in the photograph and so on.

Those days were beautiful. There was brilliant sunshine. Nazim tries to be happy, but he finds it difficult to even breathe.

It's not that, all of a sudden, the people of the town stopped wanting to get themselves photographed. It so happened that in the front portion of the first building on the street, which is an inn, a stranger, a traveller from some unknown land had appeared with a new camera. He had come to see the valley and had an excellent new camera. It had a long, protruding lens, which could capture clear pictures even of the distant snow-covered peaks. Casually, he began clicking pictures of the kehwa ghar and the lake, of the carved doorways and minarets of the mosque, of children and laughing people. Sometimes he would lie on the ground to take a picture, sometimes sit, at other times bend. Then he showed the photographs to people, all of them more lifelike than life itself, so beautifully coloured that people felt they hadn't known colours before that, so clear, so shiny that one rubbed one's eyes in disbelief.

God alone knows what kind of a traveller he was! He came to visit and stayed back permanently. He left the room at the inn and took up lodgings on the second floor of Bukhran's house. He would spend whole days in the library, then with an innocent smile on a tired face, he would show up at the kehwa ghar. Late into the night, the strains of the rabab and dilruba melded with the sound of people's laughter could be heard. Resting his elbows on the table and chin on his hands, his eyes would flash and twinkle.

It was Farrukhzad who brought the news that he had come to write a book and would stay for a year or two. Then they heard that in order to meet his daily expenses, the stranger had started clicking people's photographs, and placing people's dreams on glossy paper. Just before the hillock in the first lane on the right was Dilyaar's widow Humra's fruit shop. In one portion of that shop, he opened his studio. He would sit there until noon and then disappear into the library. When someone came to get a photograph taken, Humra would send her six-year-old son, Afsaan, to fetch him.

There was something so attractive in the stranger's face that everyone wanted to please him. Old women handed him paperbags filled with raspberries and walnuts, children gave him their milky-white sweet innocent laughter, women their hearts. Bukhran's second floor had suddenly come to life. The stranger also kept giving something or the other to people, doing small jobs for them, or he just shared with them the happiness of his heart. But often he would lock himself up in his room and not come out for days; the door to his room remained closed. Then one day, suddenly the sun would begin to shine and there would be an air of gaiety in front of the kehwa ghar, and a web of conversation would begin to spin around the stranger.

An ache rises slowly inside Nazim, then entirely envelops him, inside-out. He sighs and thinks: Humra, what enmity did you have with me? His desperation, in its madness, makes him want to go out into the street, shout and reveal the secret, that this harlot was involved with the stranger. But then he feels ashamed at his own evil thoughts. From the other side of town, where the orchards bloomed, Humra would return with her cart laden with fruit. When she would pass by Nazim's bench, she would swagger her hips and throw a lusty glance at him. All the while talking to her mule, she would carry on, then turn back, give him a saucy look and move on. At night, resting his head on his arms, Nazim would stare at the ceiling. Farrukhzad would snuggle into his chest and whisper: Everything will be all right. A cold wind would whistle outside.

The jingle of the coins in the pouch tied to Nazim's belt was getting fainter day by day. The scent of squashed leaves lying under an old old tree would assail Nazim. Once, he had seen two snakes entwined and writhing in love. There was Humra and this body of hers bursting with ripeness, sprawled on the grass, the wild, green-blue flowers of her veins snaking their way through. How, exactly how did all this happen that day? Did it really happen? There was an abundance of green in the picture, and the light was yellow. There was a body that was half hidden, the lines of what was visible nearly dissolving in the light. Her face had the blue hue of an ocean, there were two soft doves on her chest, and a soft downy nest below her navel where a small insane bird in half-a-swoon fluttered its wings. The uncontrollable bird would fly away again and again from Nazim's palms.

The photograph is hidden in the innermost pocket of the box. Its edges are fraying and its paper grimy, even though it's never been taken out since it was kept there. Sometimes, just the thought of looking at something is so much more fulfilling than actually seeing it.

Nazim would keep sitting on his bench under the open sky for days on end. The chair on which he would make people sit in order to take their photographs, remained empty. Behind the chair, the leaves of the tree were russet. Their hue brought a softness to the photographs. Would the stranger manage to conjure up this softness in his photographs? Would he be able to reproduce this romance, this mystery, this allure? Nazim would wonder—Don't people notice? A photograph is not just a photograph, there is a whole world in it.

Nazim felt as if his body was shrinking. And one day, only

his eyes would remain, eyes that would see all that no one else could. Humra, who is Farrukhzad's cousin, wanted to carry on with Nazim in spite of being married to Dilyaar. She wanted to be with different men all the time, first Dilyaar, then Nazim, then the stranger. With her youthful body as bait, she would snare and seduce men whose hunger for her body leapt like flames of a fire when fanned. The intoxicating fragrance of her body trapped you. And Nazim didn't even want to look at any other woman except Farrukhzad. But Humra wanted only to sting and bite and take revenge. And Dilyaar, who did not know anything, drowned in the well of death without ever realizing.

Nazim gently pulls Farrukhzad close. Even her breath on his face is comforting. The pouch does not jingle at all now. Nazim decides to go to the library and request Hazrat Nasruddin to employ him. He will be happy to take whatever Hazrat offers. Or he will go to the saw-mill to look for work, or to the orchards or he could even begin herding people's sheep and goats. Or he could go to the post-office and plead for work. Nazim's mind does not work any more.

Nazim had not opened his shop for three days. The camera kept gathering dust. When Farrukhzad asked him, he looked at her impassively, then went out to sit on a stone and carve rings out of a piece of wood with his knife.

Then one day, he got up and went towards the fir trees. He was missing for a whole day and night. When he returned the next afternoon, absolutely uncaring of Farrukhzad's concern, he went to lie on the bed and slept like a log for fourteen hours. Farrukhzad kept doing odd jobs here and there to put food on the table, all the while muttering under her breath. Nazim did not utter a single word. For three days, he remained silent, and then he disappeared for a whole week. Farrukhzad's face began to wilt, her eyes sank deep and her hands trembled.

Months passed. Farrukhzad gave in at first, then pulled herself together; she was despondent, then became hopeful. Nazim's shop lay empty for months.

Today the sunshine is watery again. There is a nip in the air. Strains of the rabab filter out from the kehwa ghar. Time and again, the sound of laughter bubbles up. From the side of the hillock, a mule appears on the street. Women bask in the sun on the benches near the lake. Children play. Swaddled in woollens, a baby kicks its legs in the sun.

The mule reaches the kehwa ghar. Behind the chair right opposite the kehwa ghar, the leaves of the tree are russet. A women is sitting on the chair, wearing a bright smile on her face. Sunlight is filtering through the branches of the tree onto her face. The skin of her face is coarse, as if it has been rubbed with sandpaper. In contrast, her hands and feet are sculpted and beautiful; her fingers are fine and delicate. If she were to sit in a darkened room, a yellow light would radiate from her hands and feet. But her face has definitely soaked in more years than her age. On that rough face, there is an amazing gravity which has lent it a sad beauty. A beauty that speaks of a life lived well, that knows what life is all about and in that knowing is able to respect itself. There is something tranquil about her face, grief, and a kind of joy too that comes from understanding grief and burying it deep inside.

Thick smoke emerges from the small window of the kitchen next to the kehwa ghar. Probably the stack of wood that came this time was damp. Rasool Badruddin's grating voice echoes inside. Hamdu—who not only washes the platters and cooking-pots in the kitchen but also fires the tandoor, prepares the masala for the shorba, and sometimes, when Rasool Badruddin is dead drunk, even makes hot spicy pigeon curry and a passable sheermal—listens silently to the abuses hurled at him. He does not want to remind Rasool that two days ago it was he himself who had brought this bundle of damp wood. Hamdu's wisdom is enviable in such moments. At night, it will be Rasool Badruddin who will share with him his home-made wine from a bag made from a mountain sheep's gut. There will be sips of wine with bites of sweet rotis…and then, the night shall be spent at the brothel.

Hamdu will spend the night with Kubra, the brothel's cook and maid. God only knows how Hamdu lost his heart to her pretty face and disfigured body. He will pounce on her body with the single-mindedness of a bull and soon be done with it. Tears of peaceful joy will slide down Kubra's eyes. At last, in this whole wide world, at least one man was hers. That a man's body had become one with hers will fill her with an unbounded joy. Nevertheless, Kubra will be surprised and wonder what it was in the game that made men go so crazy.

While passing through the forest just the other day, she had come across two bodies rising and falling together in one rhythm, oblivious of the world. Kubra had looked away from where she was hiding, and then as quickly, her eyes turned back and kept looking in their direction for a long time. Ornaments of flower would touch that flower-soft face and move. The scent of a wild-fruit, staggering drunk in the air. A patch of light in the layered darkness of the forest. A fairy-like face and a beautiful angel. Adam and Eve. Light streamed from their bodies and strains of music emanated in sync with their rhythm.

Kubra will lovingly caress Hamdu's sweaty hair resting on her chest and decide to cook korma for him today. And her mind will return to that glorious tableau of the forest to sneak another look.

The mule-rider dismounts when he reaches the kehwa ghar. He has a bewildered look on his face. The mule is weighed down with bags and bundles tied on either side. It squints in the sunshine as it looks around. A portion of the lake has almost frozen in the cold. The southern minaret of the library has a new coat of paint. Some old men have lit a fire and are heating stones at the entrance to a lane. When the stones are hot enough, the men will toast their frozen soles on them. Nazim looks all around. It is like watching himself meet his own self after ages.

It seems Humra's chest is riddled with holes. Dilyaar was such a strapping young man. When he would crush her in his arms, her bones seemed to break. Humra would raise her neck in pride and a rosy hue would smoulder on her skin. The sharp edges of Dilyaar's moustaches would proudly point upwards. Standing in her backyard, Humra would throw a glance outside. She had grown red flowers in stone pots, also roses on the window-sill. Humra would look after Dilyaar's house, cook for him and wash his clothes. Even Dilyaar's felt shoes would sparkle from her care.

Humra would pity Farrukhzad. God knows what kind of a husband she had got, and which world he lived in. Thank God, she hadn't married Nazim. Nazim, who once appeared in Humra's dreams. Thank God it didn't happen any more.

Dilyaar's prosperity would make her feel kindly towards Farrukhzad. It would perplex Humra, the way Farrukhzad laughed so much. What beauty radiated from her face with its prominent cheekbones. Sometimes she would look closely at Farrukhzad and try to see her through Nazim eyes.

Then she would see herself bright and chirpy in Dilyaar's laughing eyes and forget Nazim. But her body couldn't forget. There were other needs hidden deep inside which belied all her efforts. When Dilyaar had drowned, it was Nazim who had brought the lifeless body out of the lake. Dilyaar's body had swollen and turned blue. Even Nazim had turned cold blue. There were blocks of ice floating in the lake. Since that day it was as if Dilyaar's soul lives in Nazim's body.

Nazim's eyes cloud over. He has locked away all those photographs of people who would promise to come and collect them as they walked towards the kehwa ghar but never did. Some evenings, Nazim goes through them, one by one. He spreads them like a pack of cards. Behind each photograph, he seems to find a sea begin to slowly undulate, like smoke in the air. Then in the middle of the sea, the curtain of fog lifts. Nazim shuts his eyes, as if he were in a trance. His fingers feel the surface of a photograph as if it were the lowlands of snow-capped mountains, where there were no Adam or Eve, no branches, no greenery, no animal, no beast, where there were only air and earth and mountains and sky and Nazim amidst them.

By some magic, he knows that this is the world of the person in the photograph. He will stay there a while and find that behind a huge boulder the person with a snowy beard lying in a tent is the same person whose photograph he had clicked the other day. At that moment, there was the warmth of notes and coins, which he had got for selling goods, in his pocket and there was a warm smile on his face.

Or that child whose fat cheeks literally drooped from his face, whose naughty eyes wouldn't stay in one place for even a minute when his photograph was being taken, now buried deep in the ground for his mother to mourn and weep over.

And that young girl, whose face had the most amazing glow, who had come with her husband to get her photograph taken. Now her bleak, listless eyes mirrored all the lifelessness of the world as her husband had unleashed, instead of his love, his sheep-herding whip on her.

And the photograph of the forest...? Nazim trembles at the thought. Lying in the forest, watching through foliage the sharp interplay of darkness and sunlight... He feels sanity slip out of his grasp. A waterfalls tinkles somewhere in the distance. He had made love to Humra once. It was a secretive and sinful act. He had tasted the ripeness of her body, in this forest, amidst these trees, filled with the fragrance of wild flowers. The grass had been crushed under the onslaught of his passion. Light had fallen on her naked body filtering through leaves and branches just like this. Nazim hadn't lost his heart for no reason. It wasn't for no reason that he had completely forgotten about Farrukhzad for some moments.

A drowning Dilyaar clings for dear life to Nazim. The heavy overcoat that he is wearing becomes the reason for his death. It drags him down to the depths of the lake. Nazim extends one hand to save Dilyaar even as the other heartlessly pushes him away. In a frenzy, Dilyaar flings about his hands and feet with all his strength. His frantic eyes, which had brightened a moment ago at the hope of being saved, now widen in bewilderment and panic.

And then, in the throes of his last breath, Dilyaar clings to Nazim. With all his strength. A dying man's last, desperate try.

In the glacial water can be seen a piece of blue sky, a few conifers, some clouds and a little sunlight. Waterfowl, blissfully unaware of everything, cackle as they reach the shore.

'Feriza!'

Farrukhzad turns to look and smiles. The stranger calls out to her in a divinly sweet voice. There is a bundle of books in his hand. His beard is golden, as is the downy hair on his arms. He sits on a boulder by the street and places the bundle near Farrukhzad's chair.

Farrukhzad knows that he has nearly finished writing his book. She is in it, as are Nazim and the tale of Humra's disappearance, as is the town, its history, its culture, the world of the library, the minarets and the architecture of the houses.

She knows it's time for the stranger to leave. He looks towards the lake. There is a half-smile on his face.

'Feriza! Will you come with me?'

A storm slowly crosses her face. Her delicate hands flutter like caged birds on her lap.

At times, a storm rages in Kubra's mind. Why is there so much suffering in the world? She touches her body and wonders: why did this happen? This misshapen body… And Hamdu's losing his heart to it. Amidst all the gloom and trouble, such grace, such kindness... She wonders why Dilyaar died, and what happened in the forest that day—what was it? Did it really happen or was it her mind playing games with her... A trick of light in the dark? Was Dilyaar's death hidden in that light? Dilyaar, who was a great swimmer, died, and Nazim didn't? What is the fire that rages inside a human being? Why do we die when full of life and live when almost dead? The stems of the tiny flowers that she is holding in her palms quiver. While the sweet water of the blue spring keeps flowing through these mountains, and a herd of sheep, their bells tinkling, can be seen coming from afar, something snaps inside her.

Only Kubra knows that Humra, who had disappeared almost a week after Nazim, is perhaps with him somewhere. Afsaan, the poor abandoned child, is with Farrukhzad. What she had seen in the forest was so beautiful and what she sees now, so ugly, so evil.

She shivers. Heaven and hell exist at once in this world?

Nazim had the ability to see through the innermost core of the world. In the eyes of a drowning Dilyaar, he had seen a whole world. Nazim had penetrated his gaze. Thus it wasn't Dilyaar who died that day.

And after that day, the photographs Nazim clicked became lifeless. They became the record of only one moment. The faces he captured were just faces, one-dimensional; there was no depth to them any more. You placed a finger on them and realized they were just pieces of paper—not palpable as life. Something had ruptured deep inside Nazim. As if all the water of the lake had gathered heavy inside his heart. There is a river inside those who wish to see it.

The stranger collects all the photographs from Nazim's box. All of them will be a part of his book. That is the only way to save them from the world. While emptying the box, the corner of a photograph that had been tucked away to one side becomes visible. He pulls it out. It is a group photograph. It has been taken from behind. All the people of the town, together. Everyone's back can be seen. Only Nazim is visible from the front, taking a photograph.

The people in the photograph turn to look behind their backs. Humra, Afsaan, Kubra, Rasool Badruddin, Nusra Bi, Farrukhzad, Hamdu and even Dilyaar, who is dead and even after dying cannot resist suddenly appearing here and there. But it isn't his fate to escape from the picture. What is amazing is that the photograph has becomes Nazim's photograph now. A grainy faded photograph on rough paper which shows so many worlds, snow-capped peaks behind a blue lake, green trees, a herd of sheep, stones warming in a fire, old weary karkul-clad men, merry women, their pain and grief, their cheery laughter. One can see in it love that is beyond limits, heart-scorching pitiless insults, heartbreaking infidelity, the brutal obsession to kill, the obligation to go on living, the beast inside a human, the merciless desire for someone. People's whole lives and something much more than their whole lives.

*All these are stories of the photograph. It was only Dilyaar who actually died. That's all. And he died like everyone dies. The rest is fiction. The story in the stranger's book, and the stories imagined from the photograph. They say that there was really a photographer in that town, who disappeared, then returned one day many, many years later. By then, as it always happens, the world had changed.*

The mule-rider enters the kehwa ghar and wishes to address Nusra Bi as Phoophi; only no sound escapes his lips. Rasool Badruddin, who has kicked up a storm as usual, turns and asks in a cold voice: 'May I help you?'

Across the wetlands, a mad woman keeps desperately clutching any child she comes across to her bosom and screams, 'You damned child, you should have drowned in the lake with your father!'

Every time, Afsaan, startled out of deep sleep, whimpers for a long, long time.

## *The Barren Fairytale*

There is no joy left between them. Despite that, they still talk to each other as if immersed in an enchantment. They still impulsively seek each other in passion. But as soon as they begin to talk, on uttering the first word itself, they realize the futility of it: oh, what were we talking about, was there something to say really?—Like searching for loose change in the pocket, they look for words to form sentences, and after two lines, they realize they had already spoken them in the past. Then fumbling, in the stretched awkwardness of silence where they can hear only each other's breath, they sigh, sometimes in unison, and say: okay, we will talk again. Then, like strangers sharing a laughter before moving on, they go separate ways.

# FOUR

# *L'amore che*

What sort of voice was it? Like the ocean in turbulence, like a sandstorm rising up the throat. It had the sound of crushed stones; there was a wetness to it, a rough moistness. It was like lying flat and gazing at the stars in the night. It was like treading on a piece of land that belonged to some other world. As if someone had disentagled a string from the heart and pulled it into a place where the dark of the night was dimly lit by fireflies—a world of suppressed whispers. There was so much which was beyond comprehension. Perhaps a bit like a child's astonished cry when he doesn't know why he was slapped. The crying in a dream leaves behind the wetness of tears on his cheeks. His voice takes you to the painful twilight zone halfway between reality and dream. It touches the impenetrable darkness of oblivion, on whose penumbra a beam of light sparkles, brilliant, blinding. A voice whose every fibre exudes light.

His voice was like that—a whisper of the night, the caressing sound of leaves in a jungle, wood crackling in a fire—a voice I could die for. I never fell in love. The kind of love that I would forsake my life for. I listen to love songs in the grief of not having fallen in love like that. I imagine having fallen deeply in love, and perhaps feeling rough and abrasive, crooked and knotted, volatile and crazy and scattered. I imagine a love that would tremble in harsh winds but never be dimmed. But because I never fell in love, I can take the word instead, and fill it in my palms, and float it in the water. A fish swims up and immediately swallows it. I become sad, deeply sad, but it is all right… Otherwise, I could go insane listening to '*l'amore che*'.

# Rainsong

Her voice floats in a whisper towards me.

I ask: What? Come again?

Rain, she repeats.

Rain?

Then, as if teaching a small child, she repeats once again, spelling out the letters, enunciating each one slowly:

R A I N

You mean it's raining?

No, rain, she insists. This time her voice has a hint of hidden laughter.

It is dark outside and raining. A continuous sleet of dark heavy rain. And this girl is driving me crazy. God knows sitting at which end of the world, she's driving me crazy.

Are you there?

Her voice swims in the ink-blue darkness of the night. I could touch it, caress it with my fingers and fill my mouth with it and gulp it down so that it would echo inside me. Then I'd be able to know every timbre, every note, every lilt.

Before I can say another word, the phone disconnects.

Looking at the gloom in the darkness, I wonder. Can anybody have a name like Rain? It is still raining outside. Is this wrong number a dice thrown by destiny into my solitude? The smoke from the burning butt of the cigarette feels like the taste of her smokey voice.

It's broken and layered with rough undertones. Like the taste of tobacco on my tongue. Like seeing Zanzibar on the view master for the first time in my childhood. Like saying aloud 'Zanzibar' and feeling a row of goose pimples pop slowly on my skin, and making me want to speak it out loud again and again. I remember the Zanzibar view. It was a scene from a village, with a man squatting on the ground and spreading coffee beans, or maybe red chilies, don't remember which now. Beside the hut, in the background, hazily visible in the shadows, there was a cycle resting along the mud wall. But was there a cycle in reality? Or was it just a figment of my imagination? The cycle was actually not there. It was the cycle in my memory, like her voice is—in my memory.

In the dark of the night, I call out loudly: Rain! Rain!

Then I catch hold of my voice, touch it lovingly with my tongue and savouring it letter by letter, bit by bit, say once again.

Rain.

I will call three more times, and the phone will ring and her voice will whisper huskily:

Is that you? But even after calling out her name three times, the phone does not ring. I snore in my sleep and dream of rain. Then wake up in the middle of the night, distraught. I don't know why, but suddenly I think of Fae Wong. Maybe I am still in a dream.

I want to hold on to a voice and cross the desert. That voice has an echo of my mother's voice. Somewhere in a faraway playground, amidst an intense childhood game, my mother's voice would come floating across, soft and inviting, laden with the warmth of the kitchen, the aroma of freshly baked rotis with hot ghee melting on them, and the sweet smell of Ma's sweat and talcum powder. And I would, suddenly impatient, leave the game midway and run back home, my friends' imploring to get back to the game notwithstanding. Upon entering my house, I would shrug everything off. In the warm yellow light inside, Ma would turn around and smile. She would wave me off, to go and wash, then close her eyes and return to her tanpura.

In the darkness of the night, I can hear the lilting strings of the tanpura. It has been so long since Ma went away. At home, in Ma's room, the tanpura still rests in a corner in its cover with the small blue foral prints. When I go home, I play the tanpura sometimes when I miss her. My fingers caress the strings much the same way as in my childhood, when Ma would indulgently let me strum it sitting in her lap or the way she would let me wind the handle of her sewing machine.

The next time I am home, I am going to search for the Zanzibar slide and the view master. Until then, I can clearly see the coffee beans man and the Fae Wong girl whose name is certainly not Rain.

I wait in the dark for the phone to ring.

The interior of Bercos is bathed in smoke, hushed, blue and sensuous. At a table for two, I sit, quietly smoking my cigarette. No one brings me a goldfish bowl to share my solitude with. I can see a patch of the blue shirt of the girl sitting on the other side of the lounge. I can see her elbow too. Suddenly an intense yearning to touch her elbow once surges inside me. The girl gets up just as suddenly, and walks towards me. After a minute's panic, I realize that she is going towards the washroom past my table. Her hair is so straight and silky, her cheekbones so high and broad that I recall Yoko on the cover of the *White Album*. Then I remember painting with my fingers on the shoulders and arms of a girl whose face dissolves in the blue smoke. Only her clear innocent eyes remain in my memory, like the garden of sunflowers in the blue night.

The waiter has served the soup. It is as thin and mild as the light hanging overhead that wavers and fades by the time it reaches the surface of my table. I whisper slowly to myself:

> *I walked on the banks of the tin can banana dock and*
> *sat down under the huge shade of a Southern*
> *Pacific locomotive to look at the sunset over the*
> *box house hills and cry.*

The girl, while returning to her table, turns and glances at me. The light plays up her high cheekbones in such a way that I imagine she is smiling at me. I look away. At the table opposite mine sits a woman in a black blouse and black slacks. She is smoking and squinting across the cigarette smoke. The man with her is talking into his phone in soft monotones.

I have an urge to ask the head waitress to bring a goldfish bowl so that I can give it to that woman and say, 'Here! This is for you to share your loneliness with,' and then recite Ginsberg to her in my rough, low voice in order to light up a glow inside her:

> *...We're not our skin of grime, we're not our dread*
> *bleak dusty imageless locomotive, we're all*
> *beautiful golden sunflowers inside...*

In the dim, yellow light, a sunflower blooms inside me. Suddenly I am overtaken by such restlessness that a dam breaks inside me. I signal the waiter to get my bill.

He asks,

'The soup was not good, sir?'

I reply,

'The music inside me was not good, dear friend. Your soup was delicious, but please, now the bill…'

Suddenly very anxious. Some words, a sentence, a phrase do a march past helter-skelter, breaking into a sudden jig. I collect my things, mobile phone, Ginsberg's book of poems, keys, wallet, all my words, every emotion that is bubbling up my throat, choking my very being.

I write late into the night while listening to *baul* folk songs, a story that has not been written till date.

The phone rings in the night like a song. Her voice is a naughty one, snuggled in a warm blanket.

I call out, Rain?

She laughs. The horizons of a distant world are enfolded in her voice. It has the mystery of a softly padding black cat, hiding, then peeking out once in a while.

I repeat again:

R A I N?

She only laughs. God knows sitting at which end of the world, this girl is driving me crazy. I call out loudly:

Crazy crazy.

Then, in the grip of some strange elation, I listen to Spanish love songs, read poetry, and write beautiful, sad stories of solitude.

Outside, it's still raining.

# FIVE

# *Wild Green Parrots*

The path near the mango orchard looks worn. The grass has been trampled flat and it appears that not another blade will ever grow there. The earth has been rendered hard and bare. When in times gone by, the boundary wall was strong, not even a bird could enter the orchard. In the verandah next door, Eeya sits on the cot and watches the time go by. She is so old that even picking up a glass makes her hand tremble. Her skin has shrivelled up and her hair is white as cotton.

In those days, a flock of wild green parrots descended on the tip of the highest branches of the mango tree. Imprisoned in its golden cage, Mithoo would create such a ruckus. It would flap its wings in such frenzy. Or maybe it was scared. The tiled roof in the backyard has crumbled. Wild grass and shrubs have covered the ground. During the last rains, a viper had come out in the evening. It was hounded with sticks by the light of a petromax. Then, Deena had shown everyone its crushed, lifeless body draped on a thin stick.

'It was a damned poisonous snake, huzur.' His black eyes had shone.

For months after that, he continued recalling the day he had killed the viper.

At one end of the courtyard, the tubewell parapet is also in a shambles. Nobody goes that side ever since the water tap was installed. Now if somebody pumps it—and children do that often—a thin stream of ferrous, muddy-brown water comes out that tastes funny. The pipe would have surely rusted. On one side of the broken parapet, a mint creeper grows in abundance, and on the other a henna shrubbery stands proudly. Pinky grinds the henna leaves on the stone grinder on and off, picks up the paste in a saucer and with rapt attention applies a circle as big as a fifty-paisa coin or a three-leaf clover on everybody's palms. Thin as a reed, twenty-year-old Pinky has been sent back by her in-laws to her parents' house. In the afternoon, with her head bent, she cooks fish in a thin mustard paste curry and fries the fish head. Till the time the fish head is deep-fried, she sits on a low stool, hugging her knees and looking at the stove fire, thinking God knows what…

Amma takes a deep sign and says: 'Shall we get her admitted in the tailoring school? This year before the rains start, we have to get the roof tiled too, buy a new umbrella, give the fees for Mintu's school, get a prince coat stitched for Babuji, and one should go to Pinky's in-laws' house too once: they have to at least give a reason. How can anyone abandon a girl just like that?'

Her palms go damp with cold sweat and her heart beats to an unknown panic. Babuji suddenly takes the *bandi* from the hangar, silently puts it on, then goes out without uttering a word. God knows when he will return. Ever since he has been suspended from his job, he has become tight-lipped.

Supporting her waist, Eeya gets up from the cot. She bends to enter her room. After the bright sunshine outside, her eyes blink in the darkness in order to adjust to the cold dimness inside. Her thin cotton mattress and sheet are folded onto the wire cord hung across the room. There is a spittoon and a hookah next to her bed, a full-sleeve blouse and a thin-bordered sari too lie folded on the soiled pillow. Hungry, she calls out, 'Pinky, Pinky…'

There is framed photo on the wall in front of her. The owner of the house in a sherwani and achkan and a cap on his head sits on a chair. Both his hands rest on a intricately carved walking stick. Next to him is Eeya, then all of thirty years, in a sari, the anchal on her right shoulder, her hair raised in a bouffant, looking straight ahead at the camera, smiling shyly. Two plump children with a furry white dog sit near her feet. In the background a blurred visage of a huge bungalow is faintly visible.

The wild green parrots no longer descend on the tips of the branches as noisily.

# The Black Crow Woman

There was a greyish green leather-bound diary with gilt-edged pages. Like old drawers—which smell of naphthalene balls—these pages housed a secret world.

There was a man who was a father as well as a husband. Who adored his daughter, also his wife, but who was about to lose his job. Then there was this woman whose real life lay in an existence away from home. Who was only a silent shadow that haunted the house. A shadow through which the daily rituals of life passed through silently. And witnessing all this was a five-year-old girl who was growing up mercilessly fast. Who loved so intensely that her hatred surpassed her love. These three things were recorded very clearly at the beginning of the diary, and the diary was hidden away from any prying glance.

## *Entries in Green Ink*

It is nearly a year since he left. But in going away, he has come closer to me. It was not so with the others. The monotony of everyday living had blunted the edges of their love in his view. The bank and the river kept touching each other and merging so that the boundaries between love and hatred kept getting blurred; they kept trespassing on each other's territories. Therefore, his going away did not hurt them like some stab wound. But it wasn't the same for me. For me, love had stopped, as if suspended and frozen in time—the time that I last saw him. My love became a constant then, hovering above time, swirling and dancing in its pulsing intensity.

Sometimes I cry suddenly, for no obvious reason. Just yesterday, when going through old papers I came across a letter that I had written to him, tears glistened in my eyes.

It is two in the night. I can't sleep. These days if I see someone elderly, a swell of affection overwhelms me. Some unknown river of emotion bursts through my throat, catching me unawares, breaking and choking my heart. I have an intense yearning to caress any lined face, any person with a head full of white hair. Papa, there are so many things that I did not do for you, and if I could, I would do them all today.

While returning home one evening, there was this old person walking with the help of a stick. I was getting late, but I did not sound the horn. I stopped the car. He turned to look at me and then smiled looking a bit embarrassed at his handicap and also maybe with gratitude. My eyes had filled up with tears.

I wake him up. He awakens with sleep-filled eyes and in blurred tones asks, 'What happened?', then pulls me close, cuddles me with affection and says sleepily, 'Now go back to sleep.' I push him away in anger.

'Do you think I am a child? Talk to me, talk to me!' My voice rises hysterically. It stretches thin like a taut wire. He gets up, drinks water, puts his feet in the slippers and pulls out a chair in the verandah.

'Come, sit here.' He pats the seat of the empty chair beside him. The fragrance of raatrani creepers fill the night.

Moonlight filters in like a slow, surreal drizzle. There is silence everywhere. Only my erratic, angry breath talks. I hold a pulsing nerve in my palms and say: 'What do you know of love?' A drove of frightened birds shriek and chatter within me.

'Love is like a living thing. It has a life of its own.'

I don't agree with you…

A light flashes and disappears in the dark of the night. A train whistle blows through a silent tunnel. It passes on the track, making a wide, blunt noise, and the rectangular lights from its compartments trail a rushing line. Train journeys have always filled me with a deep sense of foreboding and melancholy, and also a strange kind of assurance. What is life after all if not a journey. And people who have left this world are travelling ahead of us in it. That is all. Our train has also left its station.

His voice fades. I tremble for a second. On some forgotten platform, I see a crowd of people lost to me. He is standing apart, in white clothes, laughing, the way he usually laughed. I have a glacier of sorrow inside me which melts very slowly. There is dampness inside me, some kind of sweet moisture, always.

The night's texture is something else, very different from that of the day. All things change their nature and form. The trees metamorph, the bird's chattering changes its tonal quality, as the furniture silently watch the shadows of the night. The windows shut down and a heaviness descends on the house. My happiness, too, gets shrouded in darkness just after sunset. The evenings are blue, the breath feels like it's drowning. My breath leaves my body in small gasps of panic. I feel restless in the clutch of a helter-skelter madness. Outside, the dense trees sway as a noisy flock of birds settle on their top branches.

Ayesha peeps in for a second and informs from behind the half-open doors, 'I have laid the table. May I leave now?'

In this small town, night creeps up on our rusty Victorian bungalow like a ghostly shadow. It brings along melancholy which is so palpable you could suffocate with despair. But the flavour of midnight is something else again, like the haunting melody of sarangi.

## *Entry in Green Ink*

I can feel the blisters in my soul. He laughs at me, his eyes crinkling at their edges. I feel hurt, I feel abandoned. 'You betrayed me,' I complain. My voice is a little girl's voice. I tell him, 'Always wear white.' He says, 'Little girl, comb your hair.' I wake up disoriented, feeling like a bird flying in unknown skies. He is more with me now than he ever was. His going away has in a way brought him back to me with greater poignancy. I push away the face bathed in agony and reach for the voice that always smiled.

He says that loving and liking are separate things. You can dislike someone intensely even while loving him. The way you do your parents.

When you are travelling, you are able to understand life more easily. Especially when it is raining heavily outside. I want to explain that life has no fixed rules…look how overwhelmed I feel this morning when nothing has really happened for me to feel this way—no pain, no hurt, no eagerness to reach anywhere. Whatever you say these days has no power to seduce me.

Caressing the black stripes on the coffee mug, I absently think about the long, savage, almost bestial, loneliness of daytime. If it will rain, I will watch the raindrops dripping from the leaves outside. He will come late in the night. I will restlessly march up and down the verandah. Ayesha, watching silently from inside the house, will suddenly say, 'Can I leave early tonight, bai sahib? My daughter is scared of rains.'

He had carefully kept the letters written by the ten-year-old girl. 'Dear Papa, where are you? How is the chick? Feed him broken rice on my behalf and also water the plants. The pigeon has laid two eggs here. Pinni's turtle fell in a bucket of water yesterday. He didn't die though he did turn upside down. We had to scoop him out with a mug. When will you come?'

'What is the opposite of Oedipus?' I had asked him

'Electra Complex! You are trying to psychoanalyse yourself?'

'I am reading myself these days,' I said seriously, pushing the glasses up on my nose. In the dim light of the bedlamp, his face was as if carved in stone and darkness. His shadow on the wall behind seemed totally detached from him. There was only one patch of light in the room. Sometime later he began to snore. In the dead of the night, burying my face in the book, I slowly trembled, as if my heart were filled with smoke.

He had raged at me once: 'You can never be happy.'

I had said, 'I absolutely hate my mother.'

He had said, 'You have a whole baggage of grievances.'

I had said, 'After all, when has she done anything for me? Ever?'

'You hate her because of your father.'

'I adore Papa.' I had stopped mid-word.

'How is your mother to blame for this?'

'You know nothing, understand nothing.' I was beginning to get hysterical. My mouth foamed at the corners, my body shivered with rage.

He was still calm. 'Your mother is a good woman.' That moment I hated him murderously. My heart bled. I dripped with venom. 'When I needed her, where was she? Not like Papa…'

'Your father was a dreamer.'

I had started to cry with bitterness. He didn't take me in his arms. He just watched impersonally as if judging me, and then walked out.

One day, roaming in the shrubbery behind the bungalow, I felt a sudden sense of affinity with my surroundings. Old wizened trees, stray dogs resting in the moist shadow of the bushes, and clothes hanging out to dry. The women turned to look at me with curiosity and giggled with their mouths covered when I asked them something. I had walked the whole day and returned in the evening, dust-laden and weary. He was waiting for me in the verandah, smoking his cigarette. He didn't say much. Just that I should at least inform Ayesha of my whereabouts.

Ayesha had brought a bucket of water for me to wash my feet. I had bent down to scrub the dust off my ankles and feet. Click! He took a photo of me from his cell phone. It was printed later on, but in the reckless moving of the diary from here to there the photo vanished from its pages.

I remember a photo of Papa. He was looking up in a large-framed spectacle and maybe the sudden appearance of a camera had brought a smile to his face. The picture captured him just a fraction of a second before the smile. I remember one of Ma too. But I don't want to remember the other face which was in the frame with hers.

*Entry in Green Ink*

He pulled me close, caressed my hair and kissed my forehead. I lifted my face and kissed him back, bang on his lips. He laughed, pushed me away, then immediately pulled me back and tickled my armpits playfully. My laughter brimmed over, like a river breaking its dam. I was all of five then.

'You don't like her?' His voice held a tinge of sudden understanding and knowledge.

'It's not like that, I love her.'

'Maybe, but you don't like her.'

'What are you saying!' I became defensive, then to cover up, began to laugh. 'You talk such rubbish sometimes.'

He stood behind my chair. He bent a little and gathered my hair, then softly caressed my bare neck with his fingertips.

'Listen, I have to go out for a few days. Will you be all right?'

My eyes welled up with tears all of sudden. I clasped his hands tightly. 'Don't leave me alone like this. I don't trust myself. I can endure the days alone, haven't I been doing so? But nights…'

Papa had gone far away. There were only letters. I didn't keep his letters safely. I have lost everything. Like a lost childhood, everything is gone.

He had safeguarded every letter of mine. My childish

'I-love-you-papa-dearest' cards, my scribblings, my toffee wrappers, my height charts. I would post him anything. When there were no letters, then a page from my rough copy, my drawing sheet, my pencil doodles on loose paper, small chits, anything at all.

'Little child, wear your shoes, we will go out for a walk.'

'Little child, eat your medicine. Then I will snuggle you close and make you sleep.'

'My darling little girl, my dearest darling.' He would hug me in a tight embrace and caress my hair. His eyes would fill up and a teardrop would escape the corners.

'You are crying?'

'No little child, my eyes hurt.' He would smile at me. I would touch the skin behind his ears and ask, 'You won't get old, no?'

He would reassure me: 'No, darling child, I will never grow old. See, the skin behind my ears are taut and my hair is all black.'

After that I would touch the skin behind his ears every morning to check for wrinkles. His skin was smooth. He would smile slowly and embrace me.

His skin had lost its glow. It had paled, and behind his ears were webs of wrinkles. You had lied to me, Papa.

Ma, on the other hand, glowed. She was young at every age. Ageless. Her hair was still naturally black. Her clothes were elegant and starched. She would wear thin-strap sandals and a slim bracelet on her wrists. She was very fair. Everybody took her to be my elder sister. One day she could even begin to look younger than me. She was truly beautiful, much more than me. I was more like Papa, wheatish, thin and bespectacled. My friends would become better friends with Ma than me. Papa was, in the end, my only friend. Papa who lived so far away, Papa who would smoke continuously, waiting for the train at the platform while returning back to his work after his vacations got over.

After he'd left, I would bury my nose in his pillow and smell his fragrance. In the night, I would have nightmares that he was dead. In the morning, I would get up bright and cheerful because someone had told me that the dreams we saw at night were untrue.

In the daytime, the young boy would park his bike in front of my window and sing, '... *tumko main chura loonga tumse, dil me basa loonga...*'

I would shut the windows and steal a glance towards Ma. That boy studied in Ma's college and one day I had seen him blowing a wolf whistle at her.

Our house was a house of sickly lights. Silence would hang from the corners and depression would drip down from the roof beams.

*Entry in Green Ink*

He spread the marmalade on the bread and fed me small bites. Then he wiped my lips with his fingers and commanded, 'Dream now.' I looked at him, my love shone like the sun in my eyes. The black crow cawed mercilessly from the roof parapet. I knew that he would come today, I knew for sure. In the night, there was a shower of pebbles on the window pane.

I didn't want Papa to come tonight. I was terribly scared. Ma wore a blue sari that day and her body gave off a soft fragrance. Her eyes were half closed as if she were drugged.

I felt I had to stay awake the whole night. As if my staying awake would keep away the threat. My heart beat hard in a mad frenzy. At some point, I slipped into a slumber. Around midnight, I woke up to a scream, or was it a groan…? Immediately, I heard Ma call out, 'Everything is all right, bachche. You go back to sleep.'

While looking through old documents, I had chanced upon a paper cutting, slightly torn at the edges. I could not make anything of the photo or the news item. A death, a broken life. Whose? I had no idea.

'You have to let go someday. Listen to me seriously.'

Who's this man I am spending my life with? I looked at him with wonder. 'Do you really think I am holding onto something irrelevant?'

'When will you forgive her? When she has not even done anything…?'

'You know nothing!' I was beginning to fume. Then I went quiet. How could I ever explain the soft fragrance emanating from her body. And Papa? Who was like a child before that girl child?

## *Entry in Green Ink*

He stumbled towards me, swaying. I caught hold of him and supported him. In that instant, I grew up. He was not crying, but his whole body convulsed in a dry, barren crying. I held his head as he emptied himself in the basin. The basin enamel held the remnants of his vomit in dry green patches for many days. I was no longer a child. Ma with her soft fragrance was absent from home. I had scrubbed the house clean but left the basin as it was. They were now other people, not my parents. The photo on the wall was a photo of two strangers.

His eyes were vacant now. I would caress his face and his eyes would blink with pain. He would say, 'Little child, leave me alone.'

Then he would sit with his papers late in the night. I would silently creep in and he would turn and distantly say, 'Little child, you go to bed. I have work to finish.'

I would mumble: 'I am no more a child; I am a sixteen-year-old woman, and you should also sleep now.' Sometimes he would acquiesce, at other times he would get angry.

I had removed Ma's clothes from the almirah. When she returned, there was an angry amazement in her voice. 'Why did you do this?'

'I can take care of Papa. We don't need you any more.'

'Are you mad? Don't talk nonsense!'

I had said obstinately: 'I caress his hair and he is able to fall asleep at night.'

Ma had come for only half a day. Before returning, she was in Papa's room, closeted for an hour. I paced outside like a caged lion.

That night, Papa called me to his room. 'Little child, do you have any trouble? Any complains?'

'Papa, I love you.' I had begun to weep.

Papa looked at me with barren eyes and remarked, 'Bachchi, your mother loves you.'

'And you, Papa?'

He said nothing but hugged me once and said, 'Bachchi go to sleep now.'

'Maybe you perceived the whole situation wrongly.'

I smiled cunningly. 'Okay, for once, I agree with you, but tell me, why did Papa change like that? A vibrant, loving person reduced to a shell…?'

'Perhaps he was like that, melancholic and depressive. Only you didn't know. While you live, forgiveness is a big thing.'

'You never met him. You will never understand. You can't see the child who sees the world with starstruck eyes from her father's lap. And not that woman who becomes a mother to her own father. How will you understand that he is in my blood and marrow, like I was in his.'

We had no love between us, no wisdom. We had only our complexes. That is how he explained our relationship. His fights were cold fights. The sort where you stayed emotionally apart and detached. They had the coldness and frigidity of ice. Maybe he had some elements of Papa in him. I, on the other hand, raged like a fire.

A few days ago, a snake was spotted near the banana grove. The driver and the guard killed it. Ayesha had come panting to tell me about it. I had gone out and sat on my haunches to examine the dead snake. I had gingerly touched its body. Cold, lifeless and moist. A spray of blood had congealed on its squashed hood. They had not thrown it away for quite some time. Instead, they had hung it on a stick and brought it towards the bungalow saying, 'Let's show it to sahib.'

That's what my fights with him were like. A spray of blood congealed on a squashed head.

*Entry in Green Ink*

His photograph hung in my room. Sunlight streaming in from the window would fall on it. He appeared to be smiling after all. The kettle blew small gasps of steam and the fragrance of tea spread in the room. It was same as the smell Ma wore. I took out the blue sari from the almirah and wrapped it around myself.

There was a newspaper snippet that said a seventeen-year-old minor had killed her mother. Her contention was that her mother eloped with her lover and as a result her father had died of shock.

In a half-torn picture, Ma is seen smiling with a student in some departmental function of her college.

She refuses to believe that her mother had gone to a different town on transfer. That her mother was compelled to do so since her father had lost his job some months ago and she needed to work in order to run the household. The father was mentally depressed.

I detest the psychiatrist. He treats me like a child. I am a woman, a complete woman.

He won't ever look at me. Even when he talks to me, he gazes out of the window.

Papa came again in my dreams today. He said, 'Bachchi, you are my darling little daughter.' I heard his same joyous laughter.

I look at myself in the mirror, at the pale, thin girl. There are dark circles under her eyes, and her elbow and clavicles jut out. Then I look at the woman. Her back below her blouse is vulgarly full. Her bosom is heavy. The girl undresses in front of the mirror. Her breasts are like two tiny flowers on the chest. The girl fills her palms with the flowers. Her hands are still empty. Ma is reading a book, lying on her stomach. From the wide neck of the blouse, her full breasts peep out. The girl wants to shake her up and make her get up from that obscene posture. She wants her to cover her breasts immediately. A cuss word escapes her mouth—whore!

But in reality, the girl does not utter a word. She just watches in the mirror. She can see a small portion of the window reflected in the mirror. The young boy is sitting on his bike, loafing under the tree near the gate. Papa is sitting on the verandah with a pile of papers. The lawyer says, 'Your case is weak, but I am trying my best to get you reinstated.'

Papa is so lonely. I want Ma to sit with him, to share his troubles. But Ma lies on her stomach and reads a book and the girl boils with hatred.

## *Entry in Green Ink*

Hatred is a pearl that nestles in the navel. Its fragrance spreads even if unwanted. It is a wild creeper which grows recklessly. It sprouts tiny white flowers which fall and turn into ashes. The leopard's eye shimmers in the glow of fire, its claws too. In the morning, the little bird chirping its innocence is so pure.

'Why do you keep going back to your past all the time? You know your mother sought you three times last week? She went back empty handed, disappointed.'

'And you know it's Papa's death anniversary next month?'

'The psychiatrist called. You missed your last appointment?'

'I am not benefitting from his sessions. Do you really believe that Papa's depression has seeped into me?'

I could feel the darkness raining inside me. The light inside me has fled since Papa left.

He had gone away for a week. I had asked Ayesha to stay with me.

'Sleep here in the night.'

'Bai sahib, can I bring my child too?'

While putting her daughter to sleep on the mattress beside my bed, she had turned and smiled at me, then whispered, 'This child is not from my husband, bai sahib.'

The room was dark. There was only the child's sweet breath in it. There was an inland letter on the bedside table. It had come during the day and I had still not opened it. Ma was a woman, so were Ayesha and I, and one day this sleeping child too would be one.

The greyish-green leather-bound diary, along with old newspapers and other junk, got sold to the scrapdealer. The five-year-old child suddenly transformed into a young woman. She had now come to know the psychiatrist's name. One day during the session, he had looked at her with sad eyes and said softly, 'You are a very beautiful woman.' Even her husband had said nothing like this to her, ever. That day there was a music in the way the evening descended. A blue jazz that could break your heart. The woman had said nothing. She just lay down wordlessly, tired. He also lay down beside her.

I just want to lie next to you, hold you in my arms, do nothing else and then to get up in the morning, beside you. The woman started weeping. She lay in his arms and cried. The man tasted the woman's salty tears. Then, just as suddenly, in a moment of frenzy, and as if cancelling what he had just said, he made love to her, with intense passion and with the dread of losing something unnamed.

I had said, 'Now I am better.' He had looked at me as if he were assessing something.

'You look sadder now, but also more in control, maybe…'

He stood behind my chair, gently swept away my hair, and caressing the skin on my neck behind my ears, said, 'Stay happy, always.'

In reply, I said, 'Listen, maybe you are right, I am like my mother.' Then I started to cry miserably, my whole body shaking with pain. As if I had betrayed my father again.

He gathered me in his arms, saying, 'My child, my darling child, I love you so much, so much!

I turned back, startled. Papa stood in his white clothes, smiling at me.

Ayesha's daughter chirps like a bird. Her soft baby hairs stick to her slim neck. I extend one finger towards her and she advances, stumbling on her tiny legs, then smiles shyly, turns to look back at her mother for assurance. There is a blazing red mark of a mosquito bite on her plump cheek. She sways in her baby walk and clasps my fingers tightly.

Something twists inside me. A flood of tears wells up. I want to become a child again. The child, seeing me like this, is scared. She starts crying at the top of her lungs. There is something precious inside me that has not died, and won't die.

'Be quiet, my child, be quiet, my love.'

Ayesha picks up the child, snuggles her into quietness. 'You were bothering bai sahib, haan.' She talks babytalk, soothing her and holding her tight to her chest. Resting her head on her mother's shoulders, the little doll looks at me with pure wet eyes and tear-stained cheeks.

The earth near the banana grove is moist. There is a small tap there. Some wild creepers grow profusely, tiny yellow flowers blooming on them. A few slabs of stone are kept helter-skelter beneath the tap. A bunch of grass grows tall between them. The soil is smooth and clayey. The sunlight filtering through the trees falls sweetly on this patch. As I reach the small corner of the garden, my breath catches for a minute. I stumble and a wave crawls under my skin, first of sadness, then of joy. The sunlight is tender, so pure, so true… And suddenly, a black crow lands from somewhere on the pipe.

Squatting on my haunches near the wet soil, I spread my palms open. The tap drips water, one drop after the other on them. My hands get wet ever so slowly.

# SIX

# Shahrukh Shahrukh, How Are You, Shahrukh?

## *Bed Number 42, Neuro Dependence Ward*

> *Rafael... Rafael...*
>
> *The voice was searching. In the still silent afternoon. It frenetically paced around the bylanes. It would be heard sharper when it came closer and as it became faint, Rafael understood that it had gone further away. That night in the sweat of his palms, the four shiny pebbles shone like the shining eyes of an owl.*

Holding Rafael's palms in his and massaging his wrists, Joel thinks, will he ever speak again, ever recognize me? After the wrists, he rubs the elbows, then the arms, then knees and ankles.

The doctor has advised some exercise every hour; the joints will remain flexible, it will be easier later on.

Joel looks at the wall clock. He will start the next round of exercise sharp at ten minutes past eleven. Then they will put the nebulizer and use suction to take out the cough hardened in his chest. When the nurse puts the pipe in, he grips it hard with his teeth. The nurse slaps his cheeks and says in a loud voice, 'Baba, don't grip the pipe.' Joel feels like hitting her. He can't bear to see him suffer and moves away from them.

In the adjacent bed, the child Shahrukh holds his father

in an unconscious embrace. His bandaged hands tremble on his father's back. The D ward is always bathed in a deathly silence. All the patients are comatose. Their attendants are dejected, tired, and without much hope. Outside, a shrill wail rises to a crescendo and then fades. Maybe it comes from the cardiac ward. The smell of sickness is like an overripe fruit, a bit like rotten mangoes.

On the white board, Joel reads:

Name: Rafael Tigga
Date of admission: 14 January 2008
Cause: Brain plus Hypothalamus Contusion
Procedure: Frontal Craniology
Male cath/follies: 14 January 2008
Diet…
Riley's Tube …

There are many more medical terms below, all incomprehensible. The words merge into each other and blur. Ma says she wants to come. But what will she do here? The people from the institute say that they have already spent seven lakhs on Rafael. How much more can they spend on one man. There are many more needy people who need to be helped. Father looks at me with unseeing eyes and sees nothing. Where have you gone, to which world, which is not accessible to me, where I am not required, where I can't trespass? You always did what you wanted, until the end. What am I supposed to do now, where should I go, where should I take him, in that small village near the jungles of the small shanty town of Jaspur, in that two-acre field? To that unclaimed government hospital which has no doctor?

This time it is Joel who looks outside with unseeing eyes. He sees nothing.

*Rafael makes a big splash jumping from the branch of the tree into the pond. He is a fish; his dark smooth body flashes like quick silver.*

*Rafael... Rafael...*

*The voice never leaves him. It sticks to him. He shakes his head once, and hard: oh not now, not now...*

'Sister!'

Joel is trembling with excitement. 'He just moved his head, I saw just now! You also see, sister.'

'Baba, Baba, I am Joel. If you can hear me, nod.' Joel is shaking him. After waiting for two minutes, the nurse returns to her station, bored. The squirrel on the window, startled by all the noise, raises its tail, pauses for a second, then scurries away.

The nurse is bent over bed number 44, asking, 'Shahrukh, Shahrukh, how are you, Shahrukh?'

He would have snapped out of the dream so many times, no? Rafael asks himself, scratching his neck in embarrassment every time. Every time Maria asks, 'What Rafael, you will take me to Raipur, na?'

Then Maria's black pupils dance so merrily. Her laughter is earthy, like the soil of his village, like the sweet and sour noni spinach. Her body has a veneer of salt on it. It's sensuous and lithe; no wonder all the boys in the community run after her. Rafael stands and gazes afar. He suns himself near the pond beside his fields. Lying in the shade of the huge compound wall of the mission school, he dreams. Sister Stella has promised to send him to Raipur.

Barmoo Oraon swears,

'The Christians have a good deal—catch a job in the mission and they're sorted. But where do we go? Pahan has asked for a fowl and homemade brew. Only then he will teach us black magic. He says, "Serve me first, then, will teach you how to be a bhagat."'

Then he makes an obscene gesture,

'You are one lucky bastard, man, Maria too is sweet on you, isn't it?'

Rafael neither gets angry nor loses his patience. Beneath the guava tree, a goat is slaughtered every day. Saagu Tirkey goes to the town in the mission's Jeep. Every time he blows a horn at the turning of the village. He makes some money for his evening liquor if he gets a passenger. When Father George is with him he can't afford to look for passengers, because Father talks non-stop. He takes Jesus Christ's name ten times in five minutes. He always keeps the Gideon Bible with him. And God knows what else in his white habit: cigarette, pen, watch, a small notebook, a small leather wallet. Saagu stays alert. What if Father George offers him a cigarette,. He will have to drive with one hand then. In anticipation of the offer, he practises driving with one hand all the time. Sometimes, Father asks him to stop the Jeep and takes Rafael along.

Maria says, 'When you go to the city, what will you get for me, *re*?'

'Tell me what you want, Maria.' Rafael's eyes have the waves of an entire ocean, its distant shores, its entire spread. He wants to do more for her then he is capable of. In the night, when the bela flower blooms, Rafael plays the flute, gazing at the moon. The moon melts into his veins and pulses in perfect sync with the *hum-hum* of Maria's heart. Something emanates from his body and merges with his soul. He wishes for the night to not end. The deep yearning of his soul wants it to continue beating its drum.

Father George is giving a sermon in the chapel. On Sundays, devotees crowd there to hear the story of Noah, Joshua and Moses. Lord Jesus is our shepherd and we his flock. Hearing this, Paul Tigga's daughter, Susan, starts sniggering. 'Okay, tell me, are we sheep or human beings?'

Her mother admonishes her:

'Shut up!' Then she pulls her close. The girl's been so sick for the last six months. She would suddenly turn stiff; her limbs would constrict, her eyes would turn and her body would tremble in a fit. She could die.

Sometimes, she asks Paul, 'Shall we go to the ojha, bhagat?'

He says, 'Are you crazy? If Father got to know of it, he would be mad as a herring. He will say, "Bring her to the mission hospital!"'

But Paul even hesitates to take her to the hospital. 'All right, let's do one thing, let's do what the bhagat told us to do.' He goes to meet the bhagat, making her feel like he's obliged her—*let's do as you wish.*

In the night at the edge of the forest, the bhagat lights a fire and slaughters the fowl. He pours some alcohol into an earthen pot and calls upon their God, the Maran Buru. Susan clings to her mother with a wide-eyed hypnotic stare. The bhagat touches Susan with a peacock feather, shakes it in the air and recites a mantra. His eyes are red, like hot coals. In the black night, the wind shrilly blows through the bamboo groves in the forest.

The bhagat sways in intoxication. Paul shifts from one foot to the other, remembering Father George, then shakes away the uncomfortable memory. He makes the sign of the cross on his chest and seeks a silent forgiveness from the Lord. Then he remembers his own father. In his childhood, this is how he had taken him to the bhagat when a snake had bitten him. Half his leg had turned blue and his mother had wailed, not knowing if her baby would survive. Later on, whenever Babu drank his hadia, he would blabber, 'I sacrificed ten fowls and only then were you saved…'

'I was saved and now my daughter will be saved as well. O Maran Buru, don't punish my daughter for my infidelities.'

Clamping the cleaver between his toes, the bhagat razes the head of the fowl. The fowl shrieks in a clatter and blood erupts in a shower. Susan tumbles into her mother's lap, horrified at the spectacle. Budhni gathers her trembling body and despondently looks at the dark of the night and at the burning fire. The beheaded fowl is still in the throes of death on the sand.

'Go, your daughter is cured now.' The bhagat's eyes smoulder in the light of the fire. 'Fry a barn rat's liver in spices and feed her for three days. She will be all right.'

Rafael hates all this. Every time something like this happens, there is a quarrel in the house. God knows how many times the fowl was cooked in the jungle and every time they fought over it at home. Then, Rafael told Father George all about it. That day, Father insisted on taking Susan to the mission hospital. There were worms in her stomach and she needed to take medicine for three days. She was started on the medicines, but Budhni quietly kept cooking the barn rat liver on the side.

Susan would say, 'Ma, give me some more, you cooked this so well.'

Now who knows what cured Susan, the mission hospital medicine or the sacrifice of the fowl at the bhagat, but Susan's been all right since then. Budhni looks outside, at the blue sky, and thinks it is better to have faith in both Lord Jesus and the Baran Muru. 'Who leaves their own God! Is it right to do so?' Paul admonishes.

'Afterall, they are our native Gods.'

Rafael hears the father sermonize every day. 'The English medicines and gods work fine for us.' Last Sunday, he had an upset stomach and a bout of vomiting.

'It healed with the English medicine, didn't it? I am no longer going to that fraud bhagat just to please you.'

Budhni, in her heart, silently seeks forgiveness on his behalf:

Baran, forgive him, he has lost his mind.

She will go tomorrow itself to the forest and offer the four duck eggs that she has hoarded to the bhagat as penance.

Rafael goes to his three-acre field even before the sun rises. He has passed class tenth from the mission school. After studying so much, he can't till the land any more. It is beneath him, he feels. He dreams with his eyes open. He can't sleep at night. There is nothing that holds him back, not his parents, not his siblings. There is only Maria for whom his heart yearns. He continues to pine for her even as he realizes that he will have to go to the city to fulfil his dreams. As soon as he enters Father George's room, his eyes widen as if the city has shrunk and manifested itself in the tiny mission hospital of his village. And as the city enters the ward in which his father lies comatose, his dream comes closer and closer to him; he has just to stretch his fingers and touch them. His heart beats fast like a drum in his chest and his breath stops for an instant. I will tell Maria all of this, he thinks, while lounging besides the rows of kuchia flowers in the bougainvillea-laden verandah.

Along the pharmacy corridor, Ursula sweeps the floor with a long-handled broom, three times one side, then three times the other. She hums as she works. This is her easy time when she can afford to sing, thinks a despondent Rafael. She has recently married Mangru who drives the school bus. Mangru is a tall, well-built man. The river that flows along the village, the Ichchamati, is a wide one, especially in the rainy season. Mangru can swim across it in one breath. He is known for that and also known for harpooning fishes with his arrow, for drinking a big pot of country hadia, and also for being able to eat a pot full of roasted hen fowl.

Rafael does not want to drive the school bus. He doesn't want to be the watchman at the school either. Neither does he want to be the cook at the nun's hostel nor the gardener or an errand boy at the office. His dreams are big, very big. He wants to be like Ramesar who lives two hundred miles away in another village. Ramesar passed out from the mission school and went to the city to study some more where he passed another big exam and returned to the village as a collector in an open Jeep, sporting dark glasses and wearing a colourful bush-shirt. He had come on a tour. The whole village had milled around to see him. Someone who became such a big man coming from such humble surroundings like ours. Even Father George stood up from his chair for him. I have to become like him. His breath rises in his throat, then hovers around the middle of his forehead. In the warm sunlight of the afternoon, Rafael, waiting for Father George, drifts into a stupor.

Joel watches the girl who sits holding her brother's hands. She does not talk to anyone in the ward, just watches everyone with vacant eyes. When the nurse comes to attend to the patient, she just moves away silently. The nurse does her work meticulously. She takes the temperature and blood pressure, changes the posture of the patients. In the meantime, the girl goes, stands by the window and stares outside. One day, Joel had noticed that her shoulders were heaving in a silent cry as she stood by the window. Since then, whenever the girl goes and stands by the window, Joel watches her and thinks, is she crying now? As if just his looking will give her some kind of assurance.

He turns to see that the nurse has made Baba turn sideways. He is just a bag of bones now. The skin on his face is stretched tight over the bones, barely covering them. His eyes always remain open. In the beginning, Joel often suspected that Baba was looking at him. Now he has no such hopes. Those eyes have no spark in them. The body is just an empty shell. Joel feels orphaned and hopeless.

Oh, Baba, come back, come back to us.

The doctors say nothing. Dr Mishra comes on the rounds. He is so serious that one is almost afraid to ask. The junior doctors stand in awe of him. He looks at the updates on the white board and says, stop this medicine, start that, saline water, orthopaedic socks, waterbed, and so on. The doctors and nurses stand in mute attendance. How can one ask for any information in such circumstances?

Sometimes, Dr Ahmad comes. Even the nurses joke around with him. The attendants, too, dare to ask about their patients. When he sees Joel, he pats him on the back saying, 'Pray for your father.' But how much can he pray, how much?

*Rafael looks across the fog. His soul emerges from his body and lounges around. Then it looks back at his body. With inexplicable astonishment. It looks at the sad face of Joel, looks one by one at all the six patients in the ward, and at the curly haired nurse Lata Unnikrishnan who has curved eyelashes and who stands at the nursing station writing the patients' details in the register. It gazes at the flat, laughing face of Dipanita Bora who is taking out a new bandage roll from the cupboard, and at Bijoy Barua who is hurrying into the OT wearing a green gown and a green mask. It also looks at the rows of patiently waiting attendants and their sick outside in the waiting area. It takes a round along the Pathology lab and Urology ward, smells the stale samosas and fresh tea in the hospital canteen, looks at a child with a fresh plaster on his right leg eating poori sabzi with great attention, looks at a woman falling senseless on her dead husband's stretcher. An unfathomable grief drowns Rafael, and he returns into his body and into a sleep.*

Joel picks up the bandage roll from the sidetable and wipes away the tears from the corners of Baba's eyes. Who knows how much pain is inside him. He caresses his fingers and feels as if both their bodies are one. One skin and one blood. As if just touching Baba could bring him back. So much so that he thinks that if Baba dies, a part of him will die too; it will end for ever. Something moves under his skin. At the same time, it moves within Baba in a different manner.

Joel imagines the ceiling shifting over his head. He can feel the raindrops fall on him. Don Bosco's Brother Kutty assures him that he will talk to the head office and try managing some more money. Then, giving the account, he whispers softly: 'There are others who are as needy...'

Joel counts the money on his fingers and feels a crevice open up beneath his feet. If the Don Bosco Institute had not given this money, Baba would have died that day itself. A brutal inner voice says: It would have been all right. So much expense and so much suffering. They could have saved a younger man. What will anyone get by saving Baba? He could have opened a computer shop in the city with this much money. Or one could use it to save some young man who is the provider of his family. Like Sylvarius, who was dragged hundred metres behind a truck and was still alive for one hour. Unattended, he lay in the government hospital, slowly bleeding to death. His intestines had spilled out and his blood was turning black. Even now Joel shivers remembering the panic and horror in Sylvarius's eyes. His wide-eyed terror will always remain with and haunt Joel. Maybe if he had got this money, Sylvarius would have been alive today.

Then Joel feels guilty for having such evil thoughts. He gently caresses Baba's face, pushing away his thoughts deep inside. Baba's gaze rests on him, unblinking. Joel feels ashamed and goes out. Outside, in front of a paan kiosk near the parking lot, he sits down, bereft of hope.

What did baba get after being saved that night in the fire? Sister Esther and Father Samuel died that night in such a heinous manner, so much hatred was brewing for the mission people. And why did Baba jump into the fire? For the sake of Father George? Even if he didn't get anything from the mission, was there something intangible that he received from it? The group of Bajrangis who had provoked and instigated the crowd melted away in the dark of the night, and when the police arrived, all they could see were a few foolish tribals who were promptly arrested.

The sugar-coated generosity of the mission is over. Everything is being done in self-interest now, a ploy to keep things to themselves. In the night, behind the temple, a group congregates and instigates the tribals against Father Samuel. In his white kurta-pajama, a town chap with a tilak on his forehead spreads words of hatred in whispers that ride a mad, runaway horse and go a far distance. In the dark hole, sentences drop one by one: night… that bastard Samuel… the paedophile… devilish act… to sully a child's innocence like this… the holy order… punishment punishment punishment…

Everybody gathers for karma, everybody, Hindu and Christian, all. The father at the church looks away at such times. He knows that once karma is over, the community will flock back. All those who converted did so for life, so what is there to lose now. Drum beats resound in the village the entire month. The whole jungle reverberates with joy, music and dancing. The women prepare baskets and fill it with germinated seeds for *jawa* and offer watermelon to the karam devta for fertility and birth of glorious sons. Maria decorates her basket and glancing sideways at Rafael, smiles. Rafael is in a dream.

'Will you marry me? Will you?' Maria is still smiling, but her eyes are clouded.

'Don't you trust me?' Rafael looks askance at her.

'Is this something to even ask?' Maria questions.

His face mirrors annoyance. Maria's eyes become sad. The more Rafael gets annoyed, the sadder she becomes. The drum beats differently for both of them.

In the night, Rafael thinks with astonishment: So Maria does not understand me at all, she does not know me at all. I don't want to spend the rest of my life like a sacrificial fowl hung upside down for an offering to the bhagat. I have to move away from this village, do something worthwhile. The sharp whistle of a train piercing the dead of the night pierces his heart.

*In the dream, he can see Ramesar's sunglasses. A hippopotamus lying in water enquires: 'Tell me what the businesses of the town are. Do you earn enough?' Turning sideways in the water, Rafael laughs. In the deepest part of the pond, a branch almost touches the water. He reaches to touch it once with his fingertips, then turns and dives in. Before he can complete the dive, his sleep gets disturbed.*

I have to leave for the city, I must go. Every morning, Rafael goes to Father George. He doesn't say anything, just sits silently on the verandah the whole day. When night falls, he returns home. The next morning, again he is found at Father George's. Father George watches him dispassionately, and one day, finally losing patience, he hands him a plate of chapattis and spinach when he comes in for his lunch. Rafael just nods his head in negation, without uttering a word. Four days have gone by. Father enquires in the village: 'Did he eat in the night?' Susan, Rafael's sister, informs him that he ate one chapatti in the night. Rafael remembers Gandhi baba's satyagrah. In the lamplight, he takes out the torn book from his school days and reads it.

Finally on the tenth day, at his wit's end, Father sits on his knees in front of Rafael. 'You want to go to the town? We will go day after tomorrow. Be ready, and once you are there, don't insist on coming back soon.' Father's voice turns hoarse. He doesn't remember his childhood. His face has been burnt brown and wrinkled from living here many years, and his hands have mottled.

In the night, while turning his rosary, he says a prayer for Rafael too.

In the crowded city, Rafael roams around in wonderment. Five boys are spending their days cramped in one room in the Ursine convent, eating fat brown rice and watery potato stew. Rafael has got the job of generator boy in an insurance company. When the electricity goes, his duty is to turn on the generator. He also runs small errands like taking the post and going to the bank. His freedom is gone. His heart is chained now. Sometimes he goes to the boss's house. He meets Phoolmani there. She is from his area. She is thin and small. His heart blossoms. Phoolmani is shy before him. He frequently goes to the boss's house. They share a cup of tea in front of the kitchen. He likes that. He also likes talking about Maria to her, talking about his village and his days there. That's the only thing he likes in the heartless city.

On his first vacation, he returns to the village and talks about Phoolmani to Maria all the time. He doesn't notice that Maria's face has become so small and thin, and that her eyes are so big in that face. One day before he goes back to the city, they meet in the night. The sand is white behind the dark boulders. The river reflects the moon, and in the silver night, two fish swim alongside. Rafael can't take his eyes off Maria's body. A river is born between them and slowly it runs its course and vanishes. Tears flow from Maria's eyes, endlessly.

Rafael remembers nothing of the night in the city. In the sweat and grime, the grease and noise, in the madness and the dense loneliness, Rafael sees his dream die bit by bit. He sees himself working the generator all his life. Riding a Jeep will not be his destiny. That happens only to someone like Ramesar. His own people will talk to him with condescension. The jungle is lost to him now. And the city he will never ever be able to claim.

Father George wonders: is this what I prayed for? On Sundays, he sees the despondent face of Rafael and thinks: to open a window to a world beyond someone's capacity is also a sort of crime. But to show the sky is also a sort of goodness.

Susan takes him to that curve in the river where the branches of a tree bend down to touch the water. She leads him into the water. 'Here, this is the place…' Then she moves away. Rafael watches her go. When he can see her no longer, he turns towards the flow of the water. His feet touch smooth pebbles and velvet, wet river soil. His toes search the riverbed. There must be a hole here through which Maria slipped away from this world. Then, slowly, he sits down. The water comes up to his waist. How can anyone drown in so little water? He caresses the riverbed, then starts sobbing. His tears become one with the river.

All the able-bodied boys of the village have left for the city. Some girls too. They work in offices, schools and clinics. But wherever they work, they always remain subordinate, menial, following orders and never giving them. Rafael looks with empty eyes. Every night, he dreams of money showering over his head; only all the notes are torn, not a single note is intact. A rivulet of sweat forms inside his shirt and rides his back. It never dries. *This is my destiny.*

Beneath the sal tree, classes are being held. A dozen children sway, sitting on their sacks, and recite the tables in a drone. The mission school no longer teaches poor children. Only the rich can afford to send their children there now. Rafael, with a ruler in his hand, sits on a chair, looking at the children. Bang in the centre, he can see the laughing face of Joel.

'Baba…' He puts up his small figure.

'Go, but come back soon.'

Rafael dreams again. There are many stars in the sky, but the night is no longer calm. Day and night, the noise from the quarry pervades the air. The breaking of the boulders is like a magnified wail, the roar of the beast. A layer of fine red dust covers everything, even the sky. But Rafael still dreams. Now for Joel.

> *Rafael is dancing, swirling like a spinning wheel. There is a whirlpool in the water, and in the vortex, a flower blooms that he has to pluck. Every time he reaches it, the flower moves out of his reach. Beneath his feet are the same smooth pebbles and the sticky velvet soil. He squats in the water. The water rides up to his waist, then chest, then neck. He takes a long breath, fills his lungs and, closing his nose and mouth with his fingers, dives into the water. A frenzy of bubbles rises up the river for a moment. Then the surface goes quiet. A bird flies in circles up above in the blue sky.*

Beneath the bed lying on the rug, Joel remembers his childhood. Baba had so many dreams for him. He made him study BA, sent him to the big city while working in the quarry. He filled his lungs with red dust, but what did he get? Nothing, really. Not a proper job in the mission either, same watchmanship, cleaning and being a driver, no more than that. Lord Jesus did not become our shepherd, he too abandoned us, all of us. He folds up his legs to his chest and holds them tight the way Baba held him close rocking him to sleep when he was small.

The nurse comes and shakes him: 'What happened?'

He sits up, befuddled. He realizes his eyes are wet with tears. Embarrassed, he whispers, 'Nothing'.

*Maria breathes a warm breath in Rafael's chest. Their bodies are one. Two shadows dance a tango, they separate, then merge into each other in a slow sensuous rhythm. Like a mother envelops her child in love so a cover of deep affection protects them. The skin leaves its place and the boundaries of the body melt into each other. Rafael is bent over Maria, holding her close, and Maria becomes tiny in his embrace. Yet, at the same time, she has the expanse of the ocean within her. She is so wide that her body becomes the limitless sky and Rafael a bird in it. The wind lifts their bodies up higher and higher. The night is so dark that not even a shadow is visible anywhere—only Maria's warm breath touches Rafael's chest.*

Maria's sister, Saleena, proffers the baby Joel towards Rafael. Surprised, Rafael holds the boy awkwardly and tries to find Maria's warmth in his tender body. His fingers tremble as they wander over Joel's face, his nose, eyes, lips and forehead. This was supposed to be a shared happiness. Why did Maria hold back the news from him? His eyes fill with pain as he looks at Saleena.

'You didn't come for more than a year, sent no news.'

'Yes, I didn't send news, and I didn't come. I was terribly sick, in a hospital for months, all alone. Then I had gone further than Raipur in search of a bigger dream, and in doing so, I lost Maria.' Rafael sobs, his heart wracked with pain. 'I didn't get my dream and I didn't get Maria either. I lost everything, everything.' The pain has lodged in his chest like a cough.

Since then Rafael's voice has become nasal. It comes out from within him as if fighting the cough blocking its way. People ask, hey Rafael, your cold never gets better or what, man? Why don't you take some herb from the bhagat?

Only Rafael knows that what's lodged in his chest is not a cough but Maria. Sometimes in a drunken stupor, he screams out loud:

'Maria, leave me be. I plead with you, please leave me be.'

Saleena looks at him from afar. Joel is tied to her back and they walk past Rafael, keeping a distance. Next morning, a sober Rafael turns up at her door. 'Give me my son.'

'Move away, you bastard! Get lost! You will take care of the child while being drunk all the time?'

Father Xavier has taken the place of Father George who died in his sleep one day. The mission's situation isn't good these days. The funding sources abroad are drying up. Who cares, really, whether a handful of tribals celebrate Christmas or karma!

Father Xavier talks with disdain. The people have also gradually realized that not much can come of the mission; one can't expect to go beyond being a driver or a watchman. Anger and rebellion surge within them. These days, instead of the missionaries, it's the Hindu leaders who roam about the village in open Jeeps wearing white kurta-pajamas.

Boys like Barnu and Sagu hang out with them, smoke a beedi or a cigarette and eat paan. Barnu has begun to work as an errand boy at the party's office. He always has a bundle of notes tucked in his pockets these days. Last time he even sported dark glasses when he came to Rafael to say, 'Convert to a Hindu. It's more beneficial these days.'

Rafael thinks, did my father become a Christian in his self-interest? Maybe. Then, should I reconvert to a Hindu in my own interest? What is the faith of the poor? Two whole meals a day…?

Father Xavier says, 'The mission has already done enough: sent you to the town once, got you a job. You quit and came back like a coward, so go your way now. What more can the mission do for you?'

The days pass in a haze. In the tipsiness of hadia and liquor, all dreams are smashed to smithereens. The river has dried up and flies hover over his face. Then, one day, as if waking from a drugged stupor, Rafael gets up. He wants to hold the reins of his life tight. He wants to escape the meaningless dragging down of life. And to live like he has never lived before. As if the realization has dawned that to dream a dream, you need to keep your eyes wide open, that to dream with closed eyes doesn't amount to living.

Only when you die, do you begin to live again. Living is like when after a long time of starvation, you begin gulping down food hurriedly, big fistfuls of rice and dal, so big that the food overflows from your fist and fills your throat so that you cannot breathe. That impatience is living, that satiation is living.

That night, the foxes wailed in the jungle and cold wind trailed through the bamboo trees. Rafael kept awake, huddled in his coarse blanket. All night long, he watched the dim starlit sky. His skin trembled and tingled in the cool night air. That was the night when Rafael decided there were many things that would start afresh.

The quarry work was not easy. You hit the spade so hard all day that your hands erupted in blisters and your throat got constricted inhaling the fine red dust. Your ears became numb from the noise of the crusher. The blisters gradually hardened, and now they are hard and rough as stones. When he touches Saleena in the night, he can't feel a thing, as if an inanimate thing were touching an animate one. Saleena says, 'You don't like me, do you? You married me only for the sake of Joel, isn't it?'

Rafael is no more angry about anything. He just silently looks at Saleena with calm eyes. At the quarry the next morning, he hits the stones harder. The contractor's supervisor assesses him: this man is useful, doesn't drink, doesn't talk needlessly. When Biswas, the supervisor, falls ill, his work is handed over to Rafael.

That day when the reporters came, the contractor had called him. He is our foreman, a local guy. It's our policy to employ as many locals as possible in order to make them self-reliant.

They made Rafael stand next to the crushing machine and ordered him to smile. The contractor interrupted, 'Wear this safety helmet, Rafael.'

Rafael wore it and stood next to the crusher. Four months later, the contractor showed him the magazine with his photo in it. 'See, Rafael, you are a hero now!'

Rafael wasn't stupid to be fooled by it, but he felt very good deep inside.

Joel feels very tired. So much so that even if he rests for his entire life, his fatigue will not go. Yesterday, the TV people had come. Light, camera, mike, the flashlight fell directly on Baba's face, but even in so much light, his eyes did not blink. Even in death, Baba has become a hero once again. The breaking news in the TV channel covers him, the follow-up news too. 'Four months ago, there was an anonymous attack on the Jaspur mission in which the mission hospital, the church and the nun's hostel were burnt down. The sole survivor of that attack, Rafael Tigga, is still battling for his life in the hospital. Rafael Tigga, who's been in coma for the past three months, has only his son, Joel Tigga, to attend to him. If you can recall, it was Rafael Tigga who, without giving one thought for his own life, had jumped into the inferno to save Sister Esther and Father Samuel Ekka who run the Jaspur mission. Now the church and the Don Bosco institute are dragging their feet in meeting his medical expenditure.'

The reporter's face was animated. After the recording was over, a terrified Joel pleaded, 'Could you arrange for some monetary help?' He remembered Brother Kutty's ultimatum. A man from the TV crew grimaced.

'Why don't you seek help from the people who are responsible for your father's condition?' he said with sarcasm. 'Become a Hindu!' Then he laughed obscenely.

Joel watched stunned, then looked at his father. Two drops of tears rolled out from Baba's eyes. In the square piece of blue sky visible from the window, a hawk spiralled upwards, higher and higher.

*Rafael's eyes blink in the harsh light. Father Samuel's face transforms itself into Father George's. At the end of the tunnel, in his white habit, Father stands smiling. In the background, there is so much light that everything is white and shining. Somebody nudges him from behind and asks: 'Are you a Christian or a Hindu? You have faith in the Baram Devta? Or you sing the praise of Lord God Jesus? Rafael sways. A song bursts forth from his body. The sweet smell of bread emanates from him, the green fragrance of crop floats up from his hands. He remembers the sacrifice at the Pahan's, the celebratory feast at Christmas. He remembers Maria, Phoolmani, Saleena. He remembers the tender moments, the pain and grief in his hard life. He remembers the kindness of Baram Devta, the crops growing in abundance, the graceful statue of Jesus on the crucifix, a basketful of silver fish... He remembers Sister Esther's pitiful cries in the fire at the mission, the crowd's hateful madness. What does it matter whether you are Hindu or Christian, what does it matter whether it is Christmas or karma, how to tell that it doesn't matter at all. The only thing that matters is that you have dreams in your eyes. That these dreams grow on the soil of honesty. That you have a full belly and a safe shelter to sleep, that if we have to die one day, we should live to the fullest. Something heavy shifts in his heart. Oh how to say all this…? How? How do I tell you, Joel, don't abandon your dreams, because it is through your dreams that I will dream on; inside you, I will dream, and so will my father and his father and all our forefathers. Oh Joel, how do I hold you tight to my heart.*

Rafael looks for a minute and then another, and his chest slows down—a breath goes in and remains there. Two drops of tear pause for a moment on his lids and remain suspended.

Joel is eating rice, dal and vegetables in the shanty dhaba outside the hospital with undivided concentration. This bloody hunger never leaves you alone; it takes into account nothing, no time, place, religion, caste, space and emotion. It sees nothing.

# The Enchanted Forest

## *The Prey, the Jungle and the Dry Earth*

It was the day of the Tuesday bazaar. The red-pebbled earth was wet from the night's drizzle. Drops of water still trickled from sagwan leaves. The makeshift shops sprang up, covered by blue tarpaulin. In their busy crawl, red ants drew a brown line with alacrity along the thick tree trunk. Then as suddenly they would disappear in the crumbling dust of their mole. You could even catch their bewildering jig if they inadvertently crawled up somebody's leg.

Mangru Topno, Shibu Kujur, Balu, Birsa, all of them were busy. They would hunt for small fish, mushrooms, tubers and crabs after the bazaar was over, and cook them later over the woodfire in the jungle. Then made merry over swigs of hadia, the local rice wine. But before any of that, they had to earn some money.

Mangru waits with a skipping heart, the flute tied to a slim cloth on his waist. Itwaria and Fultusia, covering their mouths with their hands, giggle shyly as they look back seeking the boys all the time. The burunsh flower stuck in the coils of their hair begins to flutter loosely above their ears. The thick silver anklets encircling their dark ankles are like lightning flashes in grey clouds. Mangru's teeth, too, shine as he smiles, like a blaze in the night.

The crowd in the bazaar swells. On the ground are spread the bounties—woven baskets, ropes, hemp trays of various shapes, bamboo brooms, tassels, conch and shell necklaces, herbs and wild spices, bunches of leafy spinach tied with thin twigs, wild plants and edible stems, fried crawlies and brown ants in leaf bowls, local sweetmeats in thick sugar syrup smattered with drowned ants, cheap watches, colourful sunglasses, printed nylon cloth and god knows what else. The pastor of the village church, Father John Ekka, taking care not to get his white robe soiled, passes by. Last Sunday, during the baptism of Maria Kujur's child, the infant had bathed the holy pastor with his piss. He had almost dropped the child in revulsion. Where was his humanity and compassion then? A group of women snigger at him as he walks past them.

The sound buzzes, moves here and there, meanders through the sheds, hovers a little bit for a while, sharp and shrill in the bargains, bickering in the intoxicated swigs of the local cheap wine, provoking and hiding in the smothered laughter, then in the dying embers of a long tiring day, defeated and flickering, restlessly shivering like the dying flame of a candle.

As the night sluggishly descends, everything winds up. The flames of the campfire reveal rectangular impressions of dismantled shops on the ground, scraps of discarded paper fluttering about in the breeze, used clay bowls and leaf plates strewn around. The jingle of coins, the fresh crackle of rupee notes pervade the air. Some people's faces look tired, sad and lost, their cracked soles are dusty. Their rubber slippers, on the desolate meandering pathways they walk, are lost and sometimes suddenly found in the silence of the forest.

The magic of the forest has vanished. It has been lost forever. The forest does not have anything to offer now. The waterholes have dried up, the granite stones spew fire, the animals have hidden themselves somewhere in the deep. It has been ages since a hunt was made. Arrows and spears are now mere toys from some bygone era. Singbonga, the Sun God, is also angry, so even rains pelt fire at them. Mundas, Kharias, Oraons, all of them look up at the sky and the sky throws down rain; clouds descend drop by drop. The darkness of the night piles up layer upon layer on the day. So much so that nothing is visible, not even your own hands. The young men of the village gulp and breathe in the darkness, the desolation, all day long and all night long. There is nothing else left for them to do. It is so dark that they cannot even see dreams. Even if Mangru plays the flute, dreams drown in the darkness.

The number of makeshift shops shrinks every Tuesday when the bazaar is set up. The city-bound trucks load gunny bags stuffed with potatoes and onions. They also carry away a few boys, their legs dangling from the back of the truck, the red dust of their land preserved under their nails. Sometimes, a couple of girls, too, hiding the tattoos on their wrists and foreheads, to work as maids, clean utensils and tidy up homes in the town. The forest of the villages has disappeared. Now the entire big city is a forest where it is man who hunts and it is man who is hunted.

*Laha pahil dharti losot ge*
*Thol thole tahekaan*
*Sekate dhati rohor ena*
*Losot haawet laagit ponkhi raja*
*Hoye mai benaw ket*
*Ona hadar hoye tege rohor ena**

---

* This Santhal vision of the physical nature of the world is found in a song sung at the manjhithan on the last day of the Karam festival.

(In the beginning the earth was a swamp
Then when did it dry up so?
That the earth should dry up
So the bird-king made the breeze
And blew it to dry the earth)

## *Today's Columbus*

The railway platform is deserted. Just outside the station master's shed, there is a lone tree that sways in the hot afternoon breeze. Its leaves fall on earth with a sad resonant music. By evening, the ground will be covered in dry leaves.

The old brown dog lays its head on its paws and observes the tree with large forlorn eyes. Then, sighing deeply, it drops its head and closes its eyes. When the train arrives, it will become alert. Then its energy will be something to watch out for. Maybe a passenger will throw a dry, stale piece of bread through the train window or maybe even a crumbly biscuit.

Behind the goods train, a thick column of water flows uninterrupted with a roar from the overhead pipe. In the corner, there is a wooden kiosk. There are jars of coloured drops, candies, lemon chews and biscuits in a row. A horde of stubborn flies madly hovers over the jars, and a moment after they are swatted, they flock back. The old shopkeeper is napping routinely and, sometimes out of habitual reflex, flits his duster to remove the flies. When the 3:40 passenger arrives, he will also be jogged out of his inertia. But in the meantime, there is long wait before the train pulls in. A few passengers, with their feet up, are napping on the only bench the station can boast off. Away from them, a woman stands alone. A child is tied to her back with the help of a yellow mark in cloth. The child, seven or eight months old, clings like a bat to his mother. In the stance of the woman, there is restlessness, apprehension, nervousness and anxiety.

Her wrists are tattooed with flowers and bang in the centre of it, in illegible lettering, a name: Bhaua Kachchap. And Bhaua Kachchap is there, standing right next to her, wearing his new terylene shirt, his hair slicked with oil, a bag slung from his shoulders. Clutched in his sweaty hands is the same flute he had played to woo Jhumki in the previous mela, when the unripe mahua was distilled, when the rice was cured to make a brew, when tipsy, he had sung while dancing madly the whole night, when Jhumki with the burunsh flower in her hair had swayed like a wild creeper to the tune of his flute. During the sarhul festival, wearing a red-bordered sari falling to their knees, the girls had held the boys by the waist and danced like a wave in the ocean, falling and rising in a tide, like a serpent dragon galloping wild in the jungle. The night, spent at the ghotul dormitory with friends, boys and girls, when the jungle, too, was a friend, when the night was a heady fragrance. Now the jungle is no more a friend, nor is the village. There is no ind now, no sarhul, no fish in the pond, no fruits on the trees. The fields are barren and the jungle escapes and hides, the black stone earth cracks, and the earth spawns fire.

The pink trunk is adorned with green creepers and flowers bought with the money hoarded since long. Jhumki and Bhaua's entire possessions are in it. Jhumki feels it with her feet every now and then, to assure herself that the tin trunk is hers and that it's safely near her. She turns her gaze towards Bhaua, lovingly looks at him, her tall, sweet-looking Bhaua. The child's tiny soft hands fiddle with her hair in sleep, his sweet raw-milk smell, his innocent fragrance, his warm weight on her back.

Who knows which train Jhumki and Bhaua will catch. But they will catch a train for sure, today itself. They have left the village on an unknown journey of exploration. They are today's Columbus.

## *The Trapped Bird*

'Where are you going, all dressed up, girl?'

'To see a film—*Bobby*.'

Saguniya smiles coquettishly. The edge of her floral nylon sari is tightly tucked at the waist and her smooth dark skin shines in the light, just like the dimmed shadow glimmering like a mirror on the dark bitumen in the sun. Birwa, tall slender, sleek like oil on water, broad-chested and long-legged, laughs, laughs and laughs.

The water flows beneath the culvert, gurgling merrily. The shadows of the distant trees shrink and blur. They tremble slowly as the leaves whisper and as darkness descends on the branches on the trunk and into the roots deep inside the soil, and flow onto Birwa's open fists and into his eyes. The jungle is now only a dream captured inside closed eyes. The sort of dream which is forbidden to visit. Forbidden to view. It is to return from this denseness to another, where pain is a naked wire along which the restless mind loiters, that Birwa lies wide-awake on the cot late into the night, his eyes seeing countless stars shining as bright as a gemstone, as sharp as the night in the forest, as the tiger's eyes burning bright, as the fins of the kewai fish flashing in the water. The heart cleaves like a tendu leaf. The village is lost, so are the homes and the people. All is gone, the breath is gone, the links are gone, all is gone.

Early in the mornings at the dhaba, his fingers shrivel

peeling a small mountain of boiled potatoes; there are so many of them that he feels *himself* turning into a big boiled potato. His fingers reek of them. The big pan stays on the stove all day long, and the tea bubbles in it, sending milk-and-tea-laden smoke up the ceiling. He noisily sips the tea that has been poured from a height into a foamy drink in the thick lined glass tumbler, and enjoys the taste. The platform near the tap has a pile of dirty pots and pans. Flies hover around leftovers, and in the open drain flow grains of rice, a discarded half-eaten green chilli, grains of black pepper, raw pieces of roti, a piece of coal and god knows what else, along with dirty water.

Blackened with oil and fat, the frying pan needs a strong, hard hand to clean it every day. A much harder hand than what he needed to chop wood in the forest when he walked with bare callused feet on the sunburnt earth and on rocks spread like a lazy black dragon. But even now, is he not burning his skin? All day long, aren't his hands and feet afire, smouldering? Just so that the utopian days return? But will they return? And if they do, for whom and for what? This village is now a village of old dying men, of lusting dissolute lads, of middle-aged drunken men intoxicated on country liquor, of bored blunt women, of barren empty land and hungry caved-in bellies, of long useless idle afternoons, of wrinkled webbed cheeks and dry vacant stumps of trees. But what is the use of pondering over these? The sun runs its course along the day, and one can gauge the time by the pile of utensils from breakfast, lunch and dinner. That is all that is left of a day for Birwa.

Saguniya would also be working as a day labourer. There is some ongoing work of a culvert on the canal. She would be carrying cement and stones, her feet sinking in the red soil and sand. As long as her waist continues to sway when she walks and her cheap anklets flash in her ankles, she will save money to watch *Bobby*, hum a sarhul song with Birwa and laugh in merriment. Who knows, while peeling the potatoes until his nails hurt, Birwa will see a new dream in which Saguniya coquettishly walks here and there, flashing a smile at him.

On her wrists are tattooed flowers, leaves and a snake. There are three black dots bang in the centre of her forehead. Also where her slanting eyes end and also on the ankles where her silver anklets rub against the feet. But Saguniya is embarrassed about the tattoos now. She wants to hide them, to erase the jungle from her memory, her body. She's in awe of the glamour of the city, its bright lights. There is such a variety of ribbons, clips, bangles, colours. Nail polish, earrings and more. The fragrance of perfume permeates everywhere, more seductive than the night of the jungle. A little bit like that Bridge babu who looks at her with his green eyes filled with a strange lust. Then Birwa's black panther, jungle eyes are lost on her. Saguniya flirts and laughs, her clothes get awry, and she moves sensuously. The Bridge babu lights up a beedi and smiles. The bird of the jungle is slowly coming, enchanted, into his web on its own. It won't be long now...

Then Birwa will look askance. One more dream will fly away from his open palms. Saguniya understands this. She knows that it's just a vibrant multi-colour dream, this glitz around her. But in reality...? In reality, the black bitumen sticks to their bodies darker than the jungle. What of the Bridge babu? A new bridge will be constructed elsewhere. Wood is being cut down in all the forests. Where will the birds go? The net has been cast wide. All the bastards will be trapped, one by one. Bridge babu laughs and the dhaba owner smirks. Birwa knows nothing, neither does Saguniya, innocent in their unawareness. But they will know one day. What will happen then?

Till that time, the magic of the jungle vanishes from their bodies, pore by pore.

# SEVEN

## *Behind the Lane*

Some old musical instrument plays. I am not able to place it, but as the night progresses, a pain courses through my veins and someone whispers to me: are you not afraid? In the floating silence, the sound of my own breathing sounds shamelessly loud and unfitting. A fragile sob breaks down, a mischievous laughter gets muffled in the middle, and someone from behind whispers to me: why do you torment me, why? The voice does not complain but holds a trace of ominous sadness, like an evening about to end.

Why does my heart go berserk every day when the evening ends? Is it the dizziness of beginning to fall from the edge of a precipice? What holds me back after all? My restlessness is a stretched wire and my heart breaks on the note of a cold sigh, or a hiccup—the cue of someone remembering me.

A lilting voice suddenly takes me back to old times, to the old affection once more. My sweet heart still beats as I walk back in time. After that closed lane there is another. One more street and I am there, and maybe you as well. Decorating my breath on the tips of my fingers, I meet you. We stumble a little in our restlessness as we walk together, or maybe my memory plays a trick on me. On a moaning and trembling note, the heart shatters, but who can see that. The water in the river flowed then and still continues to flow—how amazing that is. You tell the secrets of your heart to a friend, and once more a tinge of sadness touches me, even though you say that those days are over now, over. You laugh and, with a strange detachment, repeat: over, over.

The friend sees the colours of a fading day. She feels as if her heart is being squeezed dead, like she's on the peak of a last hiccup, senseless yet conscious.

# Darling, What Do You Know of Love?

It was a small issue that her heart didn't belong anywhere or with anyone. Inside me, a silence spiralled into a whirlwind and took my life along with it and my smile too, my faded old smile unravelled like a worn-out pullover and scattered in the air. Music, words, colours were all treasures hidden behind seven locks, as if they belonged to some other time. A weary sigh escaped her mouth for the time gone by. The sigh clutched at the fingers of some lost yearning, clawed at the wall and diminished, ashamed of its existence. Silence crawled along the corners and vanished.

A voice called from the entrance of the lane, turned around, touched the doors, peeped in from the windows and withdrew. The antique shop at the end of the lane suddenly resounded with a timbred female voice from the gramophone playing in its dark interiors. The voice was lined with suffering of the heartbreaking kind.

The shop was like a museum. Old clocks, hour glass, compass, chipped porcelain plates with gilt edges, fine bone china soup bowls, silver plates, old sepia daguerreotypes of people long gone, crocheted bedspreads and stoles yellowed with age.

The old man looks at the silence in the lane from behind his gold-rimmed glasses and listens to the gramophone. He plays the same song every day. If a customer drops by, he steps out as quickly, unnerved by the dark mustiness of the shop, into the sunny alleyway. The old man takes his watch out from his trouser pocket and checks the time. If it were twelve, a bell would ring harshly from somewhere inside. Its sound would pierce the interiors of the house, making a tunnel through its dark belly to reach him. He would go up to the back door, then come back with a bowl full of soup and, settling down in the faded armchair, drink the soup noisily. He wouldn't like anyone to disturb him during the time. Even if it were a genuine customer with his heart set on a silver key chain in the shop.

The rear side of the shop opened into a side alley. The woman would sit in between the lane and the open backdoor on a cane stool. She appeared to be working all the time. Her hands and mouth worked even if the rest of her body were in repose. Often she would sing in a thick, tone-deaf, bumbling voice, stumbling along the lyrics of the song while knitting mufflers or sometimes shawls… In summers, she would crochet laces. The old man would detachedly sit in the shop.

The woman whose photo adorned the gilt frame had a world of innocence and suffering on her face. The funny thing was that, in the photo, her shoulders appeared to be heaving in merriment while her face looked calm. Being like that was like falling down a hole where there was no division of time between night and day, and similarly between happiness and pain. For instance, when one was happy, or when happiness was about to reach completion, sadness would barge in like a flood breaking a dam, and at the peak of pain, happiness or the anticipation of it would flash in such a manner that one wondered: oh was I really sad? The face would freeze as if startled, as if mimicking itself. Also, the colours in the photo were hardly black or white. Like watercolours, they flowed into each other. As if everything was fluid and there were no defined boundaries. Like the whole universe pulsed, and at every pulsation, her face changed, her form and nature too, and the smell, the beauty, the sensuousness, everything. And this man, bending first, then standing erect, proudly walks like some caricature of an animation film whose last recourse was again to be reduced to that one cell from which its complex being had evolved; everything was so complex that it could be held together in extreme simplicity, just like a child having the seed of evil in its sweet innocence. Like the part of a body that comes alive the moment it's touched.

Many times in the night, the old man takes the photo to his room. He gazes at the face in it in the sickly light of his lamp, then sighing sadly, places it with care on the table besides. Then with the same care, he changes his clothes, folds them properly and places them at the foot of the bed. He removes his cap, wipes his head, then mumbling something like a prayer, he lies down. His eyes shed tears sometimes, but he is mostly unaware of them. His hold over his body and its various parts is weakening now, as if small kshatraps and rajas in his kingdom have risen in revolt.

The woman comes in the night to blow out the lamp. She picks up the photo and places it back in the frontal part of the house which houses the shop.

People's hearts would miss a beat and they swayed in rapture when Munni Begum sang '*Balamva tum kya jaano preet*', darling, what do you know of love… The flame in the candle holder flickered. But Munni Begum's face remained pure and unfazed, as if she had nothing to do with things like love and lust. On such a detached face, a voice lilting with poignant yearnings wreaked havoc in the mehfil.

The Almighty had given her a voice that went perfectly with her looks. It was said that when she ate a paan, one could see the juice coursing down her throat so delicate and translucent was her skin. Her diamond nose ring flashed fire when she sang. Raja sahib and Nawab sahib took a deep puff of the hookah and swooned over her. The bag of gold coins and currency notes rained on the floor. Unaware of all this, Munni Begum would start an alaap with her eyes closed and sing '*Ganga reti men bangla chhavai more raja aave lahar jamune ki…*'

Her voice was as sweet as that of a child. And when that lilting innocence combined with the coquettishness of a seductress, anyone could lose their heart. Her voice was like thick, syrupy honey, like the drugged sleep after a night of passionate lovemaking.

There was rivalry between Nawab Rifakat Ali Beg and Raja Naubahar Rai over who would seduce her first, who would be the first to open her nath. Unaware of that, Munni Begum, carefully holding the muslin odhni on her head, sang an alaap. Her innocent face flushed with the intense musical taan. 'As if the goddess herself enters her body,' so said Parbatia, the bold servant women, putting her hand to her face in awe.

Beneath the window of the first floor, a young man would stand, eyes closed, his back to the wall. He would look like he were in a trance. His feet would cramp from standing in the same position for hours, his body stiffen, but his heart would slowly begin to flow like a river. He desired for Munni Begum to transform into a small fish and swim inside his body. Both of them would flow away to another land. The anticipation of such an event filled his heart with heaviness that made him think it would break. Longlatti, Munni Begum's close confidant, would peep down from the upper storey and pity the young man. It was her compassion that led her one day to secretly take the young man to Munni Begum's room after the mehfil was over.

The old man wipes his face with the back of his hand. The edge of his shirt sleeve has become dirty. The darkness inside the shop is as soothing to him as cold moist earth. The sun outside make his eyes water. The back of his hands have a web of wrinkles, the veins have turned hard and blue and protrude unbecomingly. His skin is mottled with brown spots. There is a bell on the table in front of him. He presses it continuously in annoyance.

The woman comes out, irritable.

'You didn't give me soup today.'

The woman turns back wordlessly. Two minutes later, she brings the used soup bowl, which still has a few drops of soup at the bottom. She pushes it in front of his face: 'You remember now?' Then she turns back in anger

The old man blinks. The corners of his lips droop in silent crying. He slowly gets up, picks up the photo frame and clutches it to his heart.

The woman comes on padded feet, takes the frame from the old man and, keeping it on the shelf, leads him gently towards the chair.

On the table lie a cup of Ovaltine and two arrowroot biscuits in a plate. Hot steam rises from the cup.

'Drink this and I will get the food in half an hour.' The woman's voice is the voice of an adult appeasing a child with affection. Her hard face has softened. 'I have seen so much go unrequited and now I am tired of this whole business' is the expression on her face. Yet at the same time it also bears the softness of rain on dry hard earth.

The old man starts laughing like a child who is pleased. 'Longlatti, you are very good.' Then he gets up and plays the gramophone. '*Balamva tum kya jaano preet...*'

Munni Begum had eloped one night, carrying with her the heavy bag of old coins gifted to her by Nawab Beg. Longlatti was her ally. And one fine day, immediately after, leaving behind Zaibunisa, Khairunisa, Farkhanda, Farzanda, Longlatti, too, disappeared. Bradley Hudson had a job with the railways and it was easy to escape. They changed trains, going from one city to another: Lilua, Makhlautganj, Kolkata, god knows where all. Longlatti served them her whole life; in the beginning, Munni Begum and, after her death, Bradley sahib. But why did she spend her entire life like that, she often wonders.

While polishing the old silver utensils, she hums tunelessly, '*Balamva tum kya jaano...*' She falters at the word 'preet', coughs a bit and laughs at herself. Then she completes the song: *tum kya jaano peer, tum kya jaano peer, balamva... What do you know of pain... What do you know of pain...*

# Some Day Some Song

Ma's voice was heavy and sparkling. It had a weight and a shine. It could dive to the depths of the ocean and suddenly soar like a light feather of a bird high in the sky. My voice on the other hand was a stone sunk at the bottom of the pond. It was a voice that could move and quiver with the movement of the waves and then fall quiet in its place. When Ma spoke, her voice could wander ten rooms beyond and come back. She would carry the sharp biting cold of the winter and the pulsing heat of the summer. My voice was a tender sapling wilting in an onslaught of heavy rain. In the slow moving darkness, it heard itself and fell silent.

Ma would recount tales and laugh so much. But then, it was some other time. Ma does that no more. Ma only ponders on her sufferings now. I listen quietly. Sometimes I get tired, then feel guilty. My stories are an echo of Ma's story mostly. My memories are Ma's lost memories. I have saved carefully all that Ma has forgotten, but most times Ma dismisses my memories outright, and if I insist she gets angry, you think you can prove me wrong like this? Then, after a minute or two with a childlike innocence, she says, I remember everything, I have not forgotten any. Then to prove herself right, she recounts many incidents which for me are embarrassing to hear, like my childhood stupidities and follies.

But when Ma hums even now, the footfall of a lost time,

some bygone days can still be heard in traces. The rhythm in her voice plays hide and seek. Her voice trembles and shivers on a tightrope walk. It is like dipping one's toes tentatively in a big water tank first before entering fully. I tell everyone, Ma sang beautifully. Ma sings beautifully. Ma's voice is not lyrical soprano. Her voice is mezzo with layers. Her tone has unknown dimensions and a complex range which is more contralto. In her voice is the happiness of standing beneath a light shower, but when she opens up her voice and throws it afar, like she used to back then, it is like standing beneath a heavy waterfall and to feel the downpour in all its might and grandeur.

Ma now sings in a half-forgotten tone and falls silent. I open my voice in a lonely room, one knot, one closed nook, a filament. In it there is one element of hers, one maybe of my father who always maintained that his voice had no pitch, no bass, and one of my own. I yearn to sing, not like Ma, but like myself, in gaiety, in pain and in suffering. Behind me my daughter sings Raga Khamaj.

# *Fish Are Not Cats*

Firangi, Piere, Nero, Kalu, Lila and Panna. These names were decided. Nero in Latin meant black, so they said, though the fact was not verified, just accepted because it sounded nice on the ears. Two of them were black so they were Nero and Kalu. One was pink so she was Lila, in German, a tender pink flower. Then the one that was orange was Firangi and the yellow one was Piere—the Bhojpuri piyar which means yellow—and the last one was Panna, because I liked panna, the yellow topaz. These were our sprightly, new royal guests.

Bachchi, the kid asked, 'Can I not kiss them? Can I not hold them tight in my arms, can I not softly rub their backs?' She would instead sit with her arms around the fish bowl.

Ma would watch her in the middle of her chores. Bachchi, who could never sit still, would be calmly parked, her little chin on the table, looking into the the bowl with rapt attention. But the fish would be unaware. They swam in sync with the tune from the music player. Bachchi wanted to believe so. Her fingers tread softly on the surface of the bowl. The fish would quickly swim towards them and, just as soon, turn away.

Bachchi would lose patience and fret: 'Oh, will they ever become my pet? If I call Lila, will she come to me? Straight to my beckoning finger?'

Ma would yawn and say, 'Do you know which one is Lila?

Can you identify Firangi?' She would quietly smile to herself. Bachchi is still such a kid.

Bachchi watched and thought for a week. Then, without any hope, she said, 'Ma, how good it would be if you got me a kitten or even a puppy?'

Ma said, 'Wouldn't that upset your fish? Won't hearing you say this make them unhappy?'

In a voice laden with grief, Bachchi would answer: 'But fish are not cats, Ma.'

One day, Bachchi dipped her hand in the bowl in a bid to caress the fish. Monsieur Piere went scurrying around, Lila, the delicate fairy fish, went and hid at the bottom of the jar. Nero and darling Kalu swam in circles in panic, and Panna dearest, with her mouth gaping wide, breathlessly dashed about Bachchi's fingers.

God knows what trauma besieged her, but the next morning Firangi was seen floating stomach up on the surface. First casualty. She was decently buried in the wet soil of the big flower pot at the corner of the balcony. Now, five remained.

Lila being the pink one, and by virtue of that supposedly the closest to Firangi, was left alone, bereaved. But now it was clear that after the tragedy, Bachchi needed to be made to understand, 'Darling, dearest child, a fish is a fish, not a soft furry ball, not the sweet affectionate kitten whose touch gives a warm tender feeling. Fish give pleasure only to your eyes. They are meant to sweetly float in water, like bright butterflies flit in the air, like fairies dance and swirl in heaven. They cannot be touched.'

Perhaps we should get a cat for Bachchi. It will roam around the house in proud hauteur, and the fish will peacefully stay in their bowl. But then again, I think cat and fish make a dangerous combination.

These days, Bachchi quietly watches the fish. She has forgotten all about frying and eating up Firangi. These days, she hums a song, her lips pressed to the bowl. Piere—or is it Panna—swims towards her with its mouth agape. In that empty corner of the house, there is a lot of music these days.

# EIGHT

# Somewhere in This World

## *Why are you not playing the iktara*

Anuraj Ramdooth sweeps away the fallen leaves from the temple platform and, resting his aching back against the dilapidated pillar, sits down wearily. The harsh sun lashes his face. His canvas shoes are lined with dust. In this desolate place, this site for devotion, plundered over time and reduced to wilderness. The snake burrows and the old tree roots force themselves up and explode through its stone floor. A traveller can be seen coming from afar. He comes nearer. A scraggy goatee and drooping moustaches. He holds a stick taller than his height, bends it a bit, rests his palms over its edge and chin on his palms. He gazes at Ramdooth, his face wearing at once a guilelessness innocence and a knowing/wise smile.

The wayfarer smiles. His smile is sweet, his eyes dance in naughty merriment. Bewildered, Ramdooth speaks in the seven languages he knows. The wayfarer removes his leather slippers and stands in a corner. The slippers have his toe marks deeply embedded in the sole.

'I came the wrong way this time.' He takes a map out from his faded clothbag. 'See, I started from here, this was my route.' Then he quotes Marcus Aurelius:

> 'How quickly all things disappear, in the universe the bodies themselves, but in time the remembrance of them;

> everything which belongs to the body is a stream, and what belongs to the soul is a dream and vapour, and life is a warfare and a stranger's sojourn, and after-fame is oblivion
>
> Time is like a river made up of the events which happen, and a violent stream; for as soon as a thing has been seen, it is carried away, and another comes in its place, and this will be carried away too.
>
> Always remember the saying of Heraclitus that the death of earth is to become water, and the death of water is to become air, and the death of air is to become fire, and reversely. And think too of him who forgets whither the way leads…

'History has its own compensation, doesn't it? The wrong routes, even more so… The desert houses, hot wind and evil demons. And if a traveller encounters them, they are finished.' His voice is clear and tranquil. 'The trick to choose the right path is to keep looking for the skeletons of dead travellers to show you the way.

'I had chanced upon a map of Bartholomew Diaz's who had sailed in 1488 round the Cape of Good Hope. There was a sailor in 399 BC who was an acquaintance of Dao Jing's. The whole night, cowering from the cold wind, we had listened to his seafaring songs. We had just reached Shenzhen from Dong hawang. Our journey had just begun, and our travels seemed to endlessly stretch ahead before us. Then we came across him again at Ki Giyeh Zha. His beard had more white in it than before, and he had also learnt some more sea ditties by then. Sitting around a bushfire in Gobi desert, we had talked for long about Khotan and Pamir. Suddenly a Moor had crossed us by, half obscured in the dark of the night, and playing the same song on the rabab. He had arrived from Córdoba. He recounted tales of the heinous massacre of

Muslims and Jews after the wedding of Ferdinand of Aragon and Isabella of Castile.

'Andalusia, Constantinople, Catalonia,' Ramdooth mumbles. Then wonders in a flash, Gazipur, Ara, Hazaribag. I came just to look for my ancestors, indentured labourers who worked the sugarcane fields, Ramdooth and Ramnageena, immigrant numbers 31240 and 31241. The journey from Ara to Port Luis. And now from Quarter Borne to Bihar, Bengal.

The traveller gathers the map in his clothbag and stands up. 'I have come a few hundred years too wrong, that's all.' He says, smiling sweetly. 'It's not a big deal. The Santaragachchi railway station is milling with crowds. I will take the train going down south. And then, I'll go to Murshidabad, Bandel, Chandannagar, Nadia, Barasat, Tamluk...

'Gomez de Soto had built the church in Bandel in 1660. I will rest there for a while. Then move on to meet Joseph Francoise Dupleix in Chandernagore. Kalyan Haldar had given me his address.' He takes out a crumpled piece of paper to check the address.

Ramdooth looks at the chronograph on his wrist, the year and the moon time. The traveller has no watch on his. Instead, there is a tattoo, in Devnagri or maybe Kaithi. 'Fa Hien.'

In 399 BC. And that Spanish inquisition? That happened in the fifteenth century and, in 1730, the trading post for commerce, and the French who received the contract to trade on the right bank of Hugli from Ibrahim Khan, the nawab of Bengal. So much for the quirkiness of time...

The traveller's figure slowly diminishes in the wilderness as he walks away on the dusty road.

'Wait, wait please. At least tell me about that 1502 map, and also the ship which carried away my ancestors from their motherland to unfamiliar shores?'

'Here drink this.' I proffer the mineral water bottle towards Ramdooth. He awakens with a start, his face flushed. 'Listen, I just saw Fa Hien. He was here, asking me which century?'

'The sun has knocked your mind out. Let's move, the tyre's been replaced. What were you saying?...'

Benimadhav Ghosal is busy arguing with the driver. We have dumped our bags in the rear seat. Ramdooth returns to the crumbling temple to pick up the book he had left behind. Amidst the dry leaves, he can see an imprint on the soft soil, an impression of two feet and a round dent left by a stick, and right next to those, there are some lines doodled in the earth. In Bajjika script, it announces the arrival of coolies in 1860, *arrive des coolies' aninem, circa eighteen hundred sixty.*

'Why are you not playing your iktara?' a woman, sitting in a bus by the roadside cajoles a child who tightly clutches in his hands a ten paisa iktara. 'Why?'

## *The biggest globe ever*

We had a barometer, a lactometer and a globe in our house. There was a thermometer, too, which had broken and the mercury from it had been stored away in a tiny transparent box. We used the lactometer to check the purity of milk. We did not have a fridge back then, and Ma would boil the milk four times a day so that it would not spoil.

That the lactometer showed accurate measurement amazed us to no end. We'd triumphantly smile at each other as if it were a magic trick we had pulled off.

In the searing summer afternoons, Ma would throw aside the anchal of her sari and lie flat on the floor under the fan. While she took a nap, we would tiptoe out with the barometer. Squatting on our haunches, our feet sunk deep in the cool moist soil under a putus shrubbery, we'd read the barometer. Often we wouldn't be able to make any sense of its reading, but just seeing the reading go up and down on the scale made us feel like scientists.

Reading the globe, though, was a game of solitary pleasure. The globe was blue in colour and the earth shown in it was a pale yellow and a vibrant green. Its axis, too, was pale yellow. We would slowly spin it, close our eyes and place our fingers anywhere on it. In a few seconds, we travelled from Europe to Asia and to South America. We learnt how to reach faraway, exotic places, Lima, Peru. Istanbul and thereon to Burkina Faso, Ulan Batur, Uruguay, Samoa, Timor, Estonia, Kiribati, San Marino and so on. Then we moved on to the atlas. We'd spread it out on the floor and, heads close together, we'd pore over it, tracing our fingers on places. Then one day while rummaging through old drawers, we chanced upon a magnifying glass. It not only magnified the tiny letters on the atlas but also the lines on our palms, the pores on our skin and the whorls on our fingertips. Also, a grain of sugar on a spoon or the body of a hapless fly caught by us. Another thing: we'd converge the sunrays through the magnifying glass to focus them and burn a hole in newspapers.

But these were all second-grade games. The real fun lay in reading the atlas and the globe, in understanding the rolling mysteries of the Tundra and the savannas, in knowing about the moss, lichens and rhododendrons on the hills. It lay in lying spread-eagled, clutching the atlas to our chests and gazing at the ceiling, and while lying like that, wandering in the sun-drenched lanes of far-off places, the lanes of kahira and the Spanish crusades, and in speaking Moroccan jellaba, Arab hizab. The real fun lay in dreaming all day long.

The real fun also lay in knowing all this while geography wasn't my favourite subject in school. The blame rests with Sister Roselyn. She taught geography to my class. Her calf and ankles were slender and her instep delicate. She wore sandals with thin black straps and her feet beneath her white habit looked defenceless and innocent. When she taught temperate and Mediterranean climate, I admired her feet, her slender wrists and long fingers.

Ma sang old songs in the morning while making chapattis. A Bangla song, '*Chander hashi*' or a Bhojpuri folk song, '*Kusum rang chunri*', or else a film song, '*Rahte thhe kabhi jinke dil mein*'. She always sang as she worked. And because she worked without a pause, we could hear her singing the whole day. Her voice was layered but not sweet. I worried over it; why was it not sweetly melodious? Many times in the night, I would pray that when I got up the next morning, her voice would transform, or that I would become as fair as my Kashmiri schoolmate. Many years on, I would realize that her voice was very special. It had its own character and weight, which would make it stand out anywhere. In her voice, there was a rough timbered rhythm, a music, which could rise high and spiral itself in melody without breaking or getting scattered, which could bring the fragrance of melancholy twilight in valleys, which had an intense heartbreaking yearning in it. That my father was swept off his feet by her voice wasn't hard to comprehend. But this clarity was a thing of the future.

Ma would sleep for an hour in the afternoon. We would spend that time in the other room which was full of books. There were ten dark brown boxes, which sometimes we arranged like a pyramid placing one upon the other, four at the base, then three, then two and one at the top. All of them held books. Balzac, Proust, Zola, Flaubert, Elia Kazan, Lawrence and along with them Mahadevi, Renu, Nirala, Premchand. During the rains, the smell of wet clothes would permeate the books. Even now, the smell of rain is the smell of books to me.

We would lie on our stomachs and read books until fatigue overcame us and we fell asleep only to be woken up by Ma's singing. She would be preparing for supper then. There would be smoke outside as the night began to set in. Insects would hum and a ball of fireflies hung from the bulbs of lampposts. Our friends would have gone to their native villages for summer vacation, and as the darkness deepened, we'd be filled with a despondence we could not understand. The barometer, the broken globs of mercury from the thermometer, the globe—all would lie unattended on the shelf. Without any companions, and with only each other for company, we would be assailed by a sudden monotony. Ma's singing, too, was tinged with gloom. We would press our noses to the window panes and silently watch the dark night outside. Father, who was away for a month, might miraculously return tonight. Oh, how we hoped that he might.

Ma would boil the roti with milk. The milk would burn at the edges and the roti would become moist and soft. The whole house would fill with a sweet slightly burnt aroma. The branches of a guava tree hit the window panes in a rhythm. Ma would say, 'Eat fast, then we will go sit outside.' We would lie flat on cots and gaze at the stars. Ma would hum a bit then whisper, 'Only twenty more days. It won't be so hot then.'

Both of us would look at her and smile secretively. Father had promised to bring a big globe this time, one in which we would clearly see the smaller towns and rivers and mountains. We'd gaze at the moon and sleep would flood our eyes. Sometime in the night, a cold wind would blow and we would draw up our legs. Our bodies would shiver and our legs would come up against our chest in search of warmth. Ma would cover us with a sheet and tie up our hair with affection. We would smile in our sleep and mumble inaudibly: maybe Samoa and Timor and Lima.

## *I am not of this time*

The horse rider reins in his horse outside the tavern. Even before the deathly tired horse can take another breath, the rider wipes his dust-lined face with the back of his hand, and gathering his downcast weary shoulders, mumbles, 'I am not of this time, this time is not mine.'

In front of the stove, on the glowing coals, warming her chilled bones, she sings a song about the dreams that died an early death. She gathers the flowers born out of ashes within her heart and all the while at the bottom of the hukka, is it time that sizzles and burbles?

The Peeragadhi serai is still open at this time of the night for weary travellers.

The wide roads straddle the heart of the city, like a science fiction scene from childhood memories. Curving flyovers and dazzling neon lights hide the barren songs of their time. The rider looks in amazement at the horse's hoofs beating a tattoo on the ground. There is no dust that rises behind them.

## *Gaja in Purulia*

Half his body was obscured behind the mammoth umbrella held together by a thin wooden frame. The vehicle crossed him in a fit of acceleration, and the milky white eyes set in his astonished dark face became a blur before we went past him. Then all you saw on the roads washed in rains were groups of young girls wearing light blue shirts and dark blue narrow skirts, standing in three's and two's, and laughing in abandon, trying to keep from getting drenched.

On both sides of the road there are rows of trees. The asphalt road loses itself in a wide curve. And every time, the vehicle swallows up the road as it speeds ahead. The red soil, green trees and beyond them green, rolling fields. The air-conditioning in the vehicle belches out cold air. A sweat-drenched man on a cycle turns and looks back at us. The baby in the cloth slung on a woman's back droops in a deep slumber. These people get left behind even before they can be seen properly.

On either sides of the road through the shanty town, we see the place showcased in a row of small shops. As we slow down alongside a shop, we see jars arranged in line and on the wall behind is photo of Paramhans garlanded with a dried flower mala. Next to it is the photo of a white, mustachioed, elderly gentleman. One can also see the smoke rising from the incense on the puja rack. The car stops for a moment. From across the window, the man minding the shop looks at me with detachment. On his open arms a housefly crawls. In the jar holding the sugar candy a black ant moves continuously in a circle like any other being of this world. Rushing past us in a fuzz of disappearance are houses and people, and I think not how they live a life like this, but what would they be thinking living like this, all these people.

The driver tells us that the boundary of Bengal began at the right turn we just crossed. As if a line were drawn to mark the two states. Tribal faces and red soil this side; Bengali saris and long black hair and red sindoor that side. I wonder how it was decided that people this side would live like this and those on the other, some other way. And who would have fixed the dividing line. Where and how everybody would have automatically known that living this side, they would speak a specific language and live in a particular manner. Like so many people who divide countries, land and sea, saying, 'Look we are different from you.'

The funny thing is that the trees are bursting with green on both sides of the line. No one has told them the ritual of difference between this side and that. The roads, on the other hand, have been told. This side they are good and that side potholed. Small shops, narrow lanes, overflowing sewerage, union office, floral cotton saris hung to dry on wires in front of the houses, young lads going here and there with alacrity, yawning old men, women sitting by the streets, resting their hands on their knees, yellow boiled rice left to dry on cots alongside huts, children going to school, the electric cables strung low, railway tracks, small parcels of fields, fields and more fields and innumerable ponds…

Gosain says, 'The gaja here is very famous.' 'What else can one buy in Purulia?' I ask. 'Only gaja, what more.' He smiles, betraying his broken tooth. We see some files in the office, drink strong chai from dirty porcelain cups with little flowers on them, nibble at salty biscuits and get up to go. People peep into the small office out of curiosity. 'Come from outside, have you?'

It rains heavily on our way back. And incessantly. 'It's a Naxalite area; would be prudent to leave a bit early.' We remember the advice, but it's night and it's as if darkness too rains along with water, and we are delayed because we stopped for tea at Hindu Badshah Hotel near Jhalda. We may have to pay the price for that. But there are such big fat mosquitos around. If they didn't carry us away, what good the Naxalites can do? The rain is beating at the car panes. I look out of the window, trying to remember the names: Tati Silvey, Silli, Navadeeh, Tetla, Murree, Jhalda, Topshila, Palpal, Arhara. A taste melts in my heart, like the long lost memory of something inaccessible, unattainable. How can I have a memory of places I have never been to, a time which I never claimed, which was never mine.

While eating the Mexican prawn soup at the Mélange restaurant of Capitol Hotel, I see the tribal lad smiling alertly in his smart uniform and correcting a guest's 'melanje' to 'mélange' with politeness. I come back into the room and open the packet. I said no to the dessert at the restaurant for this. Now the gaja of Purulia will melt in my mouth, I shiver in anticipation. The cardboard box has been crushed and twisted at the corners, and the ghee has spread to its outer surface. As I open the box, a wave of disappointment assails me: this is hardly gaja, this is balushahi! Feeling cheated, I bite into one, and suddenly I am transported to another world. Contentment spreads to my very soul. The flavour of ghee mixed with the slightly smell of slightly burnt milk crumbles in my mouth. I eat three in a row, and my body sags into a stupor. I fall in sleep.

## *Where Is Your Horse, Taimur?*

The old man looks back with watery eyes at a life that has gone by. There is nothing more to do except wait. He feels as if there's a thirty-year-old young man sitting coiled up inside him. What will happen to him after his death?

We have been travelling for hours on this lonely road which meanders and gets lost among mountains. Our bodies have stiffened with fatigue. It's difficult to breathe properly at this altitude. I recall the warmth of my room in the plains. My breath comes in torturous gasps riding on the back of a faint nausea. To find a tea stall in these desolate surroundings is like finding God. Behind the stall are two barn hens and amidst them, with a splendid comb, a rooster that looks haughtily at us. The hens, like good housewives, look at us twice, then get back to picking insects off the stony earth.

The bench at the stall rests on two crooked legs and we are not sure whether we should sit on it. But on the old man's insistence, we sit down, shivering as we look lustily at the warmth of the fire and the pot bubbling merrily atop the stove kept a bit inside the shade to protect it from the heavy wind. We drink the illusory warmth from the teacups, look in turns at the mountains outside and the dirty white of the stall inside. Last year's calendar flutters in the wind that pierces through the wooden slats in the window. There's a bronze Buddha statue kept in the alcove and the smell of incense rises in a swirl before it. Compassion and benevolence shine through Buddha's slanted Mongol eyes.

Once upon a time, Tamerlane must have travelled on this route. Samarkand, Amu river and from thence to Delhi via Attock, looting and plundering the settlements, killing their population, raping their women and then, on ninety elephants, carrying away the precious stones and other spoils to build the Bibi Khanam mosque.

I love looking at maps. I keep my fingers on the map and trace the Mongol conqueror's route: Herat, Isfahan, Shiraz. What a time it would have been. It is said that Taimur or Tamer was lame. How would he have travelled? Ridden horseback with his soldiers over dreaded passes and mountains, braving the freezing winds of the foothills, and risking all. What kind of lifeforce he would have had. Raising a storm and holding their spears, gaffs and swords, their beards red with dust, holding a fire within their hearts the Arabian horses with their tight leather saddles and stirrups, foaming at their mouths, sweaty and tired. To live and to die and to live again. Nothing is wasted; one is always in search of a purpose. And the poor women, always the first victims of such plunderers. This was a way of life, so much adventure and so much suffering.

My fingers tracing the extent of Taimur's empire come back and retreat into their shells. I have touched an entire world with my fingertips. Someone had once asked: where is that fire in you? I search inside. If I have the fire, will I also become like Taimur? Will I then leave everything and wander in search of my dreams? But first I have to inspect all the nook and crannies within me, the alcoves and caves, to confront the darkness that resides in me, to remove all the pain from there so that my feet will have neither a solid floor nor any earth beaneath them. I can then spread my wings in the glittering sunshine.

There is dust on the bonnet, the rear wheel has punctured, and the spare tyre it seems had missed repair after the previous puncture. Both men are immersed in an intense debate. The old man at the tea stall watches silently through his watery eyes. His apple-cheeked daughter-in-law laughs without understanding anything.

'Any garage or mechanic?'

She spreads her palms across her mouth and laughs. The small bell hung from the rear-view mirror sways like a pendulum, then becomes still. I rescue my aching heels from the prison of my shoes and think, Taimur, where is your horse?

# NINE

## *Is It Such a Big Deal to Want to be Happy*

> *To take a photograph is to align the head, the eye and the heart. It's a way of life.*
>
> – Henri Cartier-Bresson

He always appeared to be smiling in my dreams, not in the photos.

To take a good photograph is like living a good life, to have the head, heart and eye in harmony. He looks like that in the dreams. Neither laughing nor sad, and if you stare hard enough, not even smiling.

A bit like some person whose roots have gone deep into the earth and his branches high into the sky. A bit abrasive and rough like a hardened oak, yet lighter than cotton, which lifted him higher into unbounded skies. I see the pictures taken by him. A play of light and shadow to catch the moist sadness in someone's eyes. There is desolation and intense sadness, a sadness that can cleave even the greatest happiness. A silhouette in front of light, a shadow in the dream. A soft sensuous music plays. Martha Argerich plays Schubert. He says I do not have any understanding of Schubert. I laugh, even I don't, then I become sad, very sad. There are so many things that will remain incomprehensible in this lifetime. I complain, 'Why haven't you taken any picture of mine?'

'Because there is a huge gap between your heart and mind.'

I say okay and then snap out of the dream.

He always appears to be smiling in my dreams, not in the pictures.

I want to lie on soft grass in the open rolling fields and gaze at the sky. Big things will be left out, but I want to catch the smaller ones. I want to smile in the pictures too. In reality too. Is it such a big deal to want to be happy?

# Flight

He listens to her voice with rapt attention. Sometimes when her voice crackles he strains to hear, pushing the receiver hard against his ears.

He's begun to suffer from tingling ears. It is lonely, very, very lonely. But it is a way of life and he does not think too much about it. It's of no importance at all on most days. Sometimes, like an addict, he gets throbbing pangs of desire. It balloons inside him, bulges out from his stomach, his chest, hovers around him in a hazy shimmer. It's the desire to be able to talk, to be able to hold a hand, to be able to pour a cup of tea and say casually: the flavour is just right today, to be able to say: get me a warm bottle of rum or close the goddamn door, or to be able to see a face once in a while, any face—ugly or pretty.

He looks in the mirror. A corner of it got chipped the day it was hung, like a bad omen. Tia had put small stickers of flowers along the crack to hide it. Now when he looks in the mirror he can see her, tongue out, sticking the small posies.

The sea is warm and a flock of gannets soar in the sky. Agnar goes cod fishing. He has a trawler and he sails alone. He likes to be alone. There is an expanse of blue, beneath him and above. He likes to lie down and feel the the boat rock, and to watch the blue cloud-flecked sky sway slowly, tilting to the left, then to the right. At such times, he feels he is the only one who exists in the universe. It gives him the power to become at once significant and irrelevant. Then the gannets become him and he, them. He wishes he could soar to the cliffs and swoop to the deep fjords. He wishes he could dive deep into the ocean. He wishes he were not human. And he feels that if he wishes hard, it may happen. Exhilaration lifts him up. It's a giddy feeling. He may fall from the vortex, spin out of control.

He feels guilty at affording so much pleasure. 'It is not right,' he mumbles as he feels the April sun fall warmly on his skin. He picks out a handful of raisins from his pocket and slowly chews on them, deriving the maximum juice that it has to offer. The bitter-sweet taste fills his mouth. The saliva is pungent. 'It is not right,' he repeats.

The tourists will come to stay in the cottages of Lauklines. They will drive down from Tromso. There are some scenic fjords around Lauklines. Marcus, his friend, caters to these tourists for these few months, then moves southwards to Bergen. He runs a publishing house in Bergen and moves to Vikna and Lauklines in the tourist season. Agnar lives here all the time. Tia cannot understand why he has no ambition. She would compare him with Marcus and with Jensen who is a dentist and Ragmar who runs a school. Even Agnar's sister, Ingrid, runs a catering business in Buskerud. 'Everybody moves, always.' She would say, 'I want to see the world, one country in every continent.'

Agnar wants to lie horizontal. 'I am no Viking.' He dozes off and wakes with a start. The gannets are diving deep into the water. They dive cleanly and work the surface of the white water into froth. He squints at them, then sits up. It's time to go back.

He boils potatoes to go with the poached cod for dinner and sharpens his pencils. He sketches gannets soaring in the sky, their wings stretching wide. It is dark outside. Rorvik, the main village of Vikna, is sparsely populated. His nearest neighbour is almost a mile away. He puts on the radio and listens to distant voices. When he was a child he actually believed there were miniature people living inside the radio whose sole purpose was to keep playing the songs that listeners demanded. In his imagination, they scampered across the wires, locating songs or singing them in their tiny voices. Agnar wants to be the child again who can have innocent fantasies.

The phone does not ring. He waits another hour and then, feeling defeated, calls.

Tia's voice sounds like it's separated from her body. She appears occupied. She talks as if she is talking to someone else. Funny, when she was here, she would talk to others as if she were talking to him. He would hear her talking to others and smile at the things that were meant for him. She would smile and talk all the time. Now she talks to no one. She is ill. She is in the psychiatric ward. She had slit her wrists.

'Agnar,' she mumbles, 'what will happen to you if I die?'

He lies, 'I will sit and cry and die.'

He wonders in the night, will he really die? Maybe not. Definitely not. Maybe he will pay Sula a visit, go meet her grandpa, make peace with him, maybe walk out for a smoke and maybe suddenly sit and cry in loud ugly sobs. Maybe.

A sheep bleats in the night and a dog barks. He gets up to check the latch, but pauses for a moment at the door. There is a whiff of halibut that wafts across from the shed. He didn't want to clean the devil today. It was the large one, the largest this season. They all hang in a row in the shed, the cod, the trout, the salmon and the char. It is warm now and they need to be cleaned soon.

He dreams of walking on pebbles in the clear water. The shoals are smooth on his feet. He carries the halibut in a yellow pail. When he releases the halibut in the foaming waters, the fish looks at him with round eyes and sheds a drop of blood. It rises up, clear and smooth. He picks it up. It shimmers. A dragonfly is trapped inside along with flecks of quartz. 'I will give it to Tia,' he says aloud and the morning sun kisses his eyes.

He looks up with sleep-filled eyes and says, 'Hello, is anyone there?'

A crowd of tourists passes by, shrieking and laughing. The trailer carries the fishing gear. It is still early. Agnar potters about the room. He cleans the kitchen, wipes the bathroom floor, and cooks a slab of reindeer steak. It sizzles on the hot rack. The fat in it splutters and catches a spark. The smell wafts up to the ceiling. The sweet geitost, the brown caramelized goat cheese is taken out in a platter. The rakfisk, salted trout, is sliced into thin slivers. A jug of juleol is kept ready. All this is done, meticulously, lovingly. A bunch of cream rein rose is arranged in the fat plump jar.

The windows are thrown open and one can see through them the rolling fields and the sea beyond them. In summer, it is all so beautiful and tranquil. 'It warms the cockles of one's heart.' That is what Tia would say, her blond hair, cut in a short page, flitting and whipping against her eyes in the wind. But in winters, it all turns white. The green becomes a distant memory. Tia railed against white. She bought bright red and blue curtains and hung yellow rice paper lampshades brought from Tromso. She wove a green rug and placed it beneath the fat easy chair. In the night, she would get up and say, 'The golden elk is here.' He would hear something moving outside and worry for his vats of cured fish lying out in the open. The elk never came in. One could see it sometimes, though. A dark blurred shadow would flit across the white expanse and disappear into the woods beyond.

He broods over what went on in Tia's head. Her slim taut young body. What did it feel when walking, running, sitting down in the grass, making love. What did it think seeing itself from afar? When he kissed, her mouth would be slightly acidic. When he touched her, her skin had tiny eruptions that felt rough. He loved to feel the roughness. He loved his thumb to bump a little bit. He loved to prod her swollen lips with his. She had funny swollen lips as if a bee had stung her.

She would laugh and say, 'But that's what happened when I was a little girl. I was stung by a bee.' Her face would be solemn all the while.

He didn't know what she wanted. 'I want you,' she would say and hold him tight. She would have nightmares and wake up sobbing in the middle of the night. She wouldn't let him go to the sea. She wouldn't let him go the harbour either. He would unclasp her hands and babytalk with her. He wanted to be alone. It wasn't like he did not love her. He loved her, but it was the sea that loved him more. 'I need to have the sea in my vision. I need to hear it pounding in my veins, to feel the waves roll beneath my skin. I am the golden elk. I want to live so I can die old. I want to breathe and eat and sleep. I want to be the snow, the foam, the fish and all. I want to journey in my mind, see the arctic sun and the screaming whales. The mermaid's song. I want so little…'

'Let's go to Sula. You can have the sea,' she would plead and, because he was unyielding, she would insist until an ugly row ensued. He couldn't understand what it was that they fought about.

He could see the trawlers sailing out. The sea was calm

today. He had put a sign near the fork by the road: Breakfast. He had set the table outside and covered it with a chequered cloth. He set out the food, then pulled out his sketchbook and began drawing the berries sitting snugly on the plate. He did it with a lot of patience and continued until a bunch of people trooped in out of curiosity. He served them smilingly, the cod, the meatballs and the soup. He made coffee for them and relished their enjoyment. Marcus called a few times to check if he could handle any more tourists.

It was pale-haired Jenna last season. She had come to help Marcus and, one day in the headiness of summer, he had found himself thinking more and more about her. Jenna of the long hair and Jenna of the throaty laugh. Jenna who was older and Jenna who didn't want him all the time.

Agnar feels very old sometimes. He lies down in the night and gets out of his body to examine it. The long torso, the flat stomach, the strong legs. He touches the scalp and feels the roughness of bristles near the neck. He touches the chest and tries to imagine what Tia felt while touching them. Why was she so mad about it? He can't fathom. He rouses the body and wakes it up and makes it go to the shed. He sets about cleaning the trout, char and the cod. He works through the night. The shed has to be kept clean for the fish to cure properly. He cleans the trout and char, removes the gills and guts, then rinses them one by one under the sink. That done, he scrubs clean his hands. The gutted fish is lovingly marinated in a basin of vinegar. He pauses for a cigarette, then squints through the smoke. He thinks nothing all the while. All his senses are concentrated on the pleasure of smoking. He likes working in the night. It soothes his mind and heart as well.

The vinegar is drained off and the fish now lie on a basin of rock salt, their bellies bulging out with the brine. A pinch of sugar is sprinkled on top, then a pressure is put on the fish for them to brine better. He has rows of buckets on the shelf which are about to be cured. He needs to slow down their raking by putting them in fresh brine. He shoves some of them into the freezer. In winters, he just pushes the vats outside.

He sells them by the quay side. Serving the fillets with raw onion and sour cream or mustard with dill. He loves food as much as he loves the sea. Sometimes he goes to Tromso, maybe once a month, catching the hurtigruten and getting down at the church. He visits the art gallery, sits in the church of Elverhoy and buys some Chinese souvenirs from Storgata.

Life goes on and he doesn't demand much from it. He had lost his parents at an early age in a car accident. He has no other siblings and so he inherited this house. In the tiny room upstairs, his father's fishing tackle still rests in a cupboard, as his mother's lace bedspreads lie where they do. This life is good for him.

But he can understand in a faint way that Tia needed other things. She was like a butterfly. He should stop thinking about her in the past tense. She will outlive him, he knows. She is fifteen years his junior. He is forty-two now.

He goes fishing the next day. The sea is blue and the waves are crested with white. How would it feel to close your eyes and mouth and sink deep, going straight feet down? To be in the mother's womb. He remembers reading the stories from *The Poetic Edda*, the story of Njord and Skadi. Skadi was devoted to the mountains while Njord was the sea god and because they could not decide whether to live by the mountains or by the sea, their marriage failed. Tia was a mountain goddess. He sees a face floating alongside.

The bathtub had been streaked with red. The floor was awash with pink. The smoked salmon lay mouth open on the skillet. The food on the gas stove had burnt to cinders. A full two hours had passed before she was found. Agnar had gone to see Jenna off. He had returned in his old van, late in the evening. The house had been dark and cold. It was winter and everything was shrouded in white.

He thinks about how long it takes for blood to congeal. He knows about fish blood and game blood. He guts fish and handles blood and gore all the time. But human blood? How long does it take for the body to get cold? While a person sits in the living room and downs a beer, someone else drips blood, drop by drop. He often thinks it was the dripping sound that alerted him. He insists. Though Ingrid, his sister, always counters, but that could not have been the case. He also knows that was not the case. But somewhere in his mind a trick plays and replays. The blood always drips and a butterfly always gets captured within a drop. Poor, poor Tia and poor Agnar.

But I am not poor. I am someone or something that can be a gannet. He lies in the boat that sways in the water. From the sky, the gannet looks down, stretching its wings wide. He is a tiny speck in the water, a man lying spread-eagled, almost miming the gannet's flight. The man soars high up in the blue, goes higher and higher until he is reduced to a blue pinpoint that vanishes into the deep sea.

## *One day in Marrakesh*

The parrot says, 'I write and live in some other world. If you have a life, tell me, I will write it down.'

I say, 'Go away. Somebody's life is endangered. Go away, eat your green chilli. Go pacify someone else.'

The basket vendor shrilly calls out, 'Pheasant, quail, Lalsher, mew, duck or bangles, bindis, paint and ribbon…'

The camel twists its neck and, showing all its teeth, mumbles, 'If you walk in a trot like me, one day you will reach Marrakesh.'

And I answer, 'If I have to go, why only Marrakesh.'

The parrot intervenes and points its beak to the map.

I am in the middle of an argument with myself, in the blue river of the night, looking for stars. Marrakesh. The cold wind touches my skin, the oceans, time, you…

Hands stretched, a black oil cloth covering her eyes, a small girl hops on one foot. Laughing in abandon, she reaches out to clap a hand. 'You are not supposed to think when playing my game, but it is allowed to write down everything.'

The black crow, the dark black crow, the wise old man, the wise old crow, in all its maturity, says in his deep slow voice, 'night,' and says 'day', and says 'emotions', and then 'story', and finally in the end it says 'sleep', and after that, 'awake'.

The camel clicks its fingers, bares its huge yellowed teeth, wakes up and begins to amble. Behind him, the bright orange ball of a sun dips in the ink black of the night, and the page of the calendar flutters in the air.

Waking up sleepily, I see words sitting pretty on a white paper. Writing is like making love and making love is like going to Marrakesh one day. To be in many planes in the dream time, to become someone else with you, to feel million worlds bloom inside me, to be innocent in my expectations, and to be a red chilli clutched between the beaks of the parrot, to face a thousand follies every day, so many times.

In Marrakesh a new day begins again. The camel rider wipes the sand dust from his brow, shows me a romantic dream and returns back to decorate the calendar. Tomorrow he will go to another country to be a flying kite in someone else's dream.

Q and A with Pratyaksha

P.S.

Insights
Interviews
& More...

**Q: You've been working with Powergrid as chief finance manager for many years. How did writing come about?**

**A:** Writing to me is an intimate conversation with myself. It's a way of being able to see and understand my vulnerabilities with eyes wide open. It is being with myself in such a manner that everything becomes transparent and honest. Writing is a process of descending within myself, of carrying my world in a rucksack on my back, walking through a milling crowd, of carving out an intimate space visible and known only to me. All the spaces and times that I have lived through have been stored in the deep well of memory. There is a nail on which these are hanging. Writing becomes a process of reinventing them, a process of opening new doors for myself, of living more than one life.

Writing also lends you the detachment to become an observer while going through the motions of living. It affords you fantasy amidst the routine of everyday living. It also means rushing headlong like an amateur swimmer into the deep waters. Writing for me is a stubborn effort at a constant dialogue with myself. It is like the old man riding forcefully on the shoulders of Sinbad.

Working in an office with an extremely hectic schedule robs me of the time and energy writing demands. But it also gives me a context to flee from one world to the other, both so much at variance with each other that most of the time one appears like a virtual space when viewed from the other. This gives my flights of imagination the ability to break the gravity, to fly into the unknown, to view the world with a different perception. It gives me the ease of transition; it's almost like time travel.

**Q. What were your early influences? Which Hindi writers did you grow up reading? Which world writers?**

**A:** I read all the classics early on. The literature of Qurattulain Hyder, Phanishwarnath Renu, Shiv Prasad Singh, Krishna Sobti, Nirmal Verma, Rahi Masoom Raza, Vinod Kumar Shukla, Ismat Chughtai have always enamored me. Among world writers, apart from Faulkner, Steinbeck, Tolstoy, I have also loved reading Paul Auster, Bruce Chatwin, Kapuscinski, Levi Strauss, Calasso, Atwood, A.S. Byatt, Doris Lessing; the list is endless and many times it is a particular book that has held the strings for me.

**Q. Your prose is often a series of images. It's almost like your reader is peeping through a kaleidoscope of rapidly changing scenes. Is that intentional?**

**A:** Yes, very much so. When I write I paint visuals. My images are like pebbles glittering in the sand along the river. Their texture, their feel, their colour, present before me a maze of intricate paths through which they have travelled through mountains and plains to reach me. I mostly draw a curtain, hiding the obvious. My worry is how to satisfy the creative yearnings arising within me. Like the different genres of painting which use different mediums to express ideas, I too constantly search for new mediums to write. The stories are the same. It is just the way of telling that is different.

I love the way the fast-moving pace creates an impressionist image. It is blurring the reality, smudging the lines so that each scene merges into the other and when, hopefully, the reader is done, he will carry a taste or a visual of something that is not overtly definable. At least that is what I strive for.

**Q. Let's come to the structure of your stories. Scenes don't necessarily or apparently merge into each other. The plot doesn't have a beginning, middle and end. What's your view on the design of a short story?**

**A:** Writing is not only a physical act but also a metaphysical one. The rhythm follows its own pattern. The story finds its own narrative style. When I am writing, the discovery or invention of an emotional landscape appeals to me much more rather than a conventional story structure with a proper beginning, middle and an end. A slice of life which has all ends open attracts me more because life is after all like that, full of possibilities and hope.

When I write, my heart meanders into the intricate pathways of layered emotions. I am not interested in obvious straight narratives. I like it when any writing creates a space for its readers from where their imaginations can take a jump, where they can claim the story as their own. If even one sentence opens up ten windows, that makes my writing worthwhile. And because that is my expectation as a reader, that is what I strive to write too. A world full of mysterious allusions, a world full of intricate possibilities, a world full of things which are not right or wrong but just exist as they can.

**Q: Let's come to the story 'The Black Crow Woman' with the girl suffering from Electra complex in it. Did you ever know a girl like that? And why such a title – 'The Black Crow Woman?'**

**A:** The girl has some shades of people I know. Perhaps she has some shades of me as well. When I write, I dredge out a lot of memories: of people, places and time and, in some strange alchemy, all these fuse together with my imagination to become a character or a situation.

I like the girl for the way she loves her father. She is intense and protective of him. She thinks she can create a complete world for him. There is nothing physical or sexual in her yearning for him, I know that for sure. But then deliberately in my writing, I keep that as a hint, like a veiled secret hunger. I give my readers a freedom to go in that direction too. I am opening another window for them. And that is where my pleasure in writing this story comes from.

This story was titled 'Kenchul' in Hindi, which literally means snakeskin. But as I wrote it, the image of a woman draped in black kept flashing in my mind's eye, and the crow on the water tap in the end of the story too. These images were so strong that I felt they symbolized the dark secret passion the story is about. 'The Black Crow Woman' reflects the corrosive emotion, the deep wail in the throat that is lodged for years and which you can't get rid of.

**Q: You draw a lot from nature. Where did you spend your growing-up years? Did you ever meet or get to see people like Jose Tigga and Rafael Tigga. Also, there is politics in some of your stories but very understated. Perhaps you use it just as a device to convey human condition; is that right?**

**A:** I spent my childhood mainly in Ranchi where I studied till class twelve in Sacred Heart and Nirmala College. My father, who was in the Bihar Administrative service, would get transferred every two years, and we would spend our vacations in lovely small-town places like Madhepura, Chaibasa, Chakradharpur, Sasaram, Simdega…

I spent time climbing trees, flying kites, playing with a peg top, staying in dak bungalows, looking at coal-laden trains, riding cycles in hot afternoons, reading books smuggled in tin boxes amidst sugarcane fields at a friend's backyard. All these are now distant memories, and sometimes I am not even sure whether they all really happened or not.

Then the time spent with people like Jose Tigga. These tribal people are my own. They are tied to me by the umbilical cord of childhood days. Rafael Tigga is so close to me. He is like my own father in coma. The closest that I feel to any character in my book.

The political understatement is always there. In all our lives. In the environment that we live in. I feel obsessed with all that is wrong in this world. It breaks my heart to be part of it and to be not able to do anything concrete about it. It is a sort of impotent rage and constantly reduces me to shamefulness. One day I know I am going to write very strongly about it.

**Q: Love and its complexities populate your writing. Tell us about some of people in this book whose love disturbed you as you were writing their stories?**

**A:** Love brings in a lot of pain. It has the power to take you to a frenzied pitch. But it is never serene at its peak. And that lack of serenity has the power to intrigue me always.

I find Longlatti very intriguing. I connect with the character in 'I Am love'. It touches my heart to feel the love of Jose for his father Rafael in 'Shahrukh…'.

The complex layering of emotions in 'The Invisible Alley' was for me a journey of unravelling my own emotions bit by bit, like going on an archeological expedition.

The five characters in 'Five Tales' are each a small nugget of emotion polished and brightened. But above all, the complex emotions of 'The Whispering Magic of the Jungle' are closest to my heart. It is not a conventional love story between a man and a woman but a love that mankind feels for his surroundings, for nature, the earth and the sky and all the elements. And the tragedy of losing all that is the greatest tragedy that can strike mankind. It is the larger picture that haunts me constantly.

**Q: Which of your characters are closest to your heart? Tell us why.**

**A:** Rafael Tigga is closest to my heart. In him I see all that is good that can be found around us and also all the frailties and vulnerabilities within us. He is the idealist and he is the practical practitioner of life, the humble stone crusher, the ordinary generator boy who dreams big, who loves with calm serenity, who gets broken but rises always. Whenever I think of him, I get a lump in my throat.

He is a real person about whom I know nothing. I saw him in the Neuro Dependence ward in Apollo hospital, Ranchi. His face rose in front of me, and I created a character superimposing on the real one. In that sense, he is my father who lay in coma in the same hospital. The spirit that I created in him is the spirit of my father who was an amazing person. And I wrote him with all the grief, sorrow and love that I had within me.

Then the writer in 'Rainsong'. He is a person who is on

the threshhold. For whom everything is waiting to happen. He perceives the world with a childlike wonder and innocence. I wish for that spirit in all of us. The creative anticipation that catapults you into a space of blue lights and smokey whispers, of kaleidoscopic colours and vibrant music. He is a bit like anyone being in the '*Lucy in the sky with diamonds*' state of being.

And, of course, the friend in 'I Am love'. I wrote his character with all the empathy and wisdom that I have within me. He is the sweetest note in my writing – the river flowing calmly, the silver strain in the rocky mountain face.

**Q: How does the Hindi world perceive your stories; I mean your contemporaries and seniors?**

**A:** I have two anthologies published by Bharatiya Jnanpith and Harper. Two more are due to be published this year by Aadhar and Rajkamal Prakashan. The one that is coming from Rajkamal is very close to my heart, a trip away from the conventional. A sort of prose-poetry story.

I have had seniors talking positively about my writing, about the way I use language as such, about my craft and the way I present a narrative. A lot of love has come my way from my seniors, contemporaries and readers, responses that have touched my heart, reviews that have given me great joy.

However, one thing that is extremely important to me when I write is that whether *I* am happy with it or not, whether the process of writing satisfies my creative cravings or not. If that happens, everything else is like icing on the cake.

**Q: *Rainsong* also contains some of your prose pieces interspersed with the stories. Could you briefly explain why or how they have been grouped together in the nine parts that make this book.**

**A:** It is like plating the food. A process to enhance the aesthetic, visual and sensual feeling. The prose pieces are interspersed with stories following a pattern. The nine sections have one long story arranged around two or three prose pieces of similar flavour so that when the reader is going through them, he can get an enhanced taste of each one of them. Sometimes the prose pieces are like preludes to the main story, almost like the alaap before a bandish. And sometimes, it is like a dessert after the main course. All the prose pieces are small insights into life, fleeting emotions that capture the essence of life – a bit like salt in the food.

I am constantly alluding to food because I feel that these pieces are exactly like hors d'oeuvre. They add to the piquancy, aroma and flavour of the main course. They are sharp and insightful and whet your appetite.

They are in a way miniature paintings and, in their own way, complete the canvas of my writing. They are more honest and real than the stories that I write. It is also in them that I can play with words and the construct of sentences. I can take the liberty of jumping from one emotional landscape to another and, because they capture a moment of happiness or sadness, they stand out more poignant and vibrant, more sharp and clear. They have finer brush strokes in them, delicate handling, fragile texturing. The stories and the prose pieces thus create a spectrum of intimate landscapes.